DOCTO

Staff Nurse Lynne Howard loves her work in the
Casualty Department of St David's Hospital, until
circumstances catapult her into a compromising
situation with Senior Casualty Officer Timothy
Layton.

# DOCTORS DON'T CRY

BY

ELIZABETH GILZEAN

MILLS & BOON LIMITED
London · Sydney · Toronto

*First published in Great Britain 1971*
*by Mills & Boon Limited, 15–16 Brook's Mews,*
*London W1 1DR*

*This edition 1983*

© *Elizabeth Gilzean 1971*

*Australian copyright 1983*
*Philippine copyright 1983*

ISBN 0 263 74179 6

03/0183

Set in 10 on 11 pt Linotron Times

*Photoset by Rowland Phototypesetting Ltd
Bury St Edmunds, Suffolk
Made and printed in Great Britain by
Richard Clay (The Chaucer Press) Ltd
Bungay, Suffolk*

# CHAPTER ONE

LYNNE Howard heard the clock on St David's tower strike two and hastened her steps towards the Casualty Department. As staff nurse it wouldn't do for her to be late on duty. It was all the fault of the unexpected sunshine. It had tempted her to linger among the glories of the late chrysanthemums and the Michaelmas daisies. It was like an extra bonus after a chilly beginning to September. She had other reasons for lingering. Matron had told her this morning that she would have top priority when the time came in the spring to replace Sister Casualty. The older woman was retiring and Lynne knew she would be groomed by an expert for a smooth takeover at Easter. Of course, under the rules there would be other candidates for the position, but obviously the matron of St David's Hospital didn't anticipate any opposition to her plans.

Lynne rounded the corner of the Casualty wing and idly noticed that an ambulance was revving up for departure. A sudden shout startled her and she saw someone in a white coat beckoning furiously.

Lynne gulped slightly and hurried forward. She saw to her dismay that it was Timothy Layton, Senior Casualty Officer, and the expression on his face suggested that he hadn't been enjoying the sunshine. The ambulance moved forward slowly and Timothy Layton's long arm whipped out and hoisted Lynne into the ambulance as if she had been a naughty toddler. The ambulance doors slammed shut and the vehicle gathered speed.

As Lynne collected her wits she saw that two awestruck junior nurses were staring at her. She choked back her angry retort and managed to ask quietly:

'Where are we going, Dr Layton—if it isn't a secret destination?' The anger in the Casualty Officer's face told her that she had chosen the wrong moment to assert herself.

'It's a *four-ambulance alert*, Staff Nurse. There's been a roof collapse at the underground extension. The call came in at five to two.'

Lynne didn't bother to remind him that she hadn't been due on duty until two o'clock precisely in any case. This wasn't the time to bother with personal trivialities like the feud between Timothy Layton and herself. She turned to the juniors and carefully checked the emergency equipment with them. It was their first major emergency and she could guess at their fears. She gave her instructions in a low tone and ignored Timothy Layton's conversation with his medical students. She knew they were supposed to work as a team, but co-operation was difficult when it all had to come from one side.

The ambulance was moving swiftly now, threading its way through knots of late lunch traffic by judicious use of its siren, and now and again using a side street as a short cut. Then abruptly they were there. Lynne saw the giant crane lifting aside enormous blocks of tumbled masonry with an expert gentleness that seemed oddly at variance with its size. There were small tense groups of workmen removing débris with the feverish intensity of threatened tragedy. The three other ambulances were already there, their occupants standing ready for a chance to use their equipment. As the St David's ambulance came to a standstill Lynne guided her juniors out and waited quietly for the Casualty Officer's instructions.

With a muttered word to his medical students to stay

where they were, Timothy Layton strode forward as swiftly as the rough ground would allow. Lynne watched him talking earnestly to the head of the rescue operations, and wondered miserably why she always managed to put a foot wrong, without even trying, where the Casualty Officer was concerned.

There was a sudden stir among the workmen as the crane lifted a slab of concrete and revealed a gaping hole. A shouted command and all work stopped. The roar of London traffic filled the silence and the whine of a jet overhead brought back a note of normality to the scene.

Timothy Layton was back with them before Lynne had time to gather her scattered thoughts.

'There are four men trapped in there—at least one of them is still alive. I'm going in. Staff Nurse, I'll need your assistance. Bring the small drum of emergency equipment.' He waved aside the medical students' eager offer of help and didn't seem to notice that Lynne's hands were shaking as she picked up the drum and followed timidly at Timothy Layton's heels like a reluctant puppy.

All her life Lynne had had a horror of dark confined spaces, and even at twenty-three the thought of entering that jagged hole made her feel suffocated. Her training held her steady as the foreman gave her a steel helmet in exchange for the frilly cap of a St David's staff nurse. Someone in the group chuckled as she floundered about in the large wellingtons they insisted she must wear over her shoes.

An angry murmur from the Casualty Officer reminded them all of the urgency of the situation. With a swift gesture Lynne rejected the boots and followed Timothy Layton in the direction of that jagged hole. Emergency lighting had been rigged up and Lynne could see that inside the opening everything looked reassuringly normal—just like the earlier television news pictures—the preformed lining seemed unbroken with no alarming bulges.

Timothy Layton was arguing with someone in charge. 'No, there's no point in your men coming with us. I'll call you back on this—' he patted the bulge of the intercom in his top pocket. 'You won't be able to move the trapped man until I've seen how badly he's injured.'

Once again he gestured impatiently to Lynne and she followed him into the gaping tunnel. For the moment it seemed less frightening in the glare of the lamps at the entrance. There was a distant throbbing which Lynne guessed must be the pumps in another section. They sounded like the beating of a giant heart. Lynne's shoes slithered a little as the ground sloped slightly. If Timothy Layton hadn't been in such a hurry back at St David's she would have collected her own wellingtons from the plaster room.

Just ahead of her Timothy Layton's voice echoed eerily and it took her a moment to realise that he was speaking into the intercom and not to her. 'There seems to be a roof fall in one of the side openings. Were Jenkins and his gang working in the main tunnel? Over.' There was a crackling sound and then the thin voice of the unseen operator. 'They could have been, sir, but my guess is that they were on their way back. Jenkins might have spotted something—say water dripping—and gone to investigate. His speaker seems to have gone dead before we could get much detail. I'll call you back—over.'

Lynne almost dropped her precious drum as another voice spoke out of the darkness of that side opening. 'Cut that cackle and get me out of here, guv, and make it snappy. The other blokes must have copped it. Mind how you go. Hang on until I shines the lamp on you.

Crikey! What you got Florence Nightingale here for? Don't you know that all hell's due to break out any sec?'

Lynne felt like crying out that she wasn't any Florence Nightingale and never even wanted to come in the first place. But Timothy Layton gave her no time to think.

'Watch how you go, Staff Nurse.' He grabbed at her as she slipped on the mud. 'Why haven't you got your boots on, you silly little fool?' Characteristically he gave her no chance to answer. 'Get the morphia syringe ready. Well, Jenkins, where are you hurt?'

'Back and legs mostly, Doc. Here, take my lamp and have a dekko.'

Lynne shuddered as the light revealed a jumble of mud and masonry out of which emerged the head and shoulders of a very large man whose tousle of fair hair fell over blue eyes that blinked in the glare and then steadied. 'Looks a bit frightening, eh, Nurse? Now, you take my advice and trot back up the tunnel and get yourself out of here. Take no heed of your boss, miss. He should be ashamed of hisself a-bringing you at all.'

The Casualty Officer was curt. 'Save your breath, man. Give me that syringe, Staff Nurse. Careful now, don't drop it.'

Lynne had time to admire the deftness with which Timothy Layton made the injection. Then came a dull rumble and then a rush of air followed by a blackness that pressed smotheringly down upon her. She felt something move and reached out blindly for it, to feel her hand grasped by another hand—an enormous one.

'Steady on, lass. At least it's not on top of us this time. Where's the doc got himself to? Hey, Doc! You playing games with us?'

But there was only silence, a stillness punctuated by the occasional slither of a pebble or the fainter drip of water, and the heavy breathing of the big man who held her hand so gently. Lynne must have made some panicky movement.

'Don't worry your pretty little head, Nurse. My mates don't give up easy. The light should be somewhere close. Guess I dropped it. Hang on, I've got it.'

The sudden brilliance made Lynne screw up her eyes. Slowly and reluctantly she opened them, terrified of what she might find—Timothy Layton buried under débris, themselves in a small dark hole. Reality was almost more frightening. A mountain of sticky mud had blotted out the way back to the comparative safety of the main tunnel. A few more pieces of masonry had joined the jumble and within arm's reach lay the huddled body of the Casualty Officer. His safety helmet had fallen off and the bright light revealed a nasty bruise over one temple.

Gingerly Lynne scrambled to her knees and crawled over to Timothy Layton. It only took a brief examination to warn Lynne that she no longer had a boss to tell her what to do. He was deeply unconscious and she could count on no help from him for quite a while. As she checked his pulse Lynne felt the coldness of his wrist. She would have to do something fast for Timothy Layton or else she and Jenkins would be on their own.

As she ran her hands over his body to make sure there were no other injuries, her fingers encountered the bulge of the intercom in the Casualty Officer's top pocket. Quickly she drew it out and crawled back to Jenkins.

He gazed at her drowsily and she realised the morphia injection was taking effect. 'What you got there, Nurse? Found the doc, have you?'

Lynne took a deep breath and licked her lips. 'Dr Layton has been knocked out, Mr Jenkins. I'd better let them know what's happened.'

The big man stared up at her, his blue eyes beginning

to look glassy as the drug dulled his senses. 'You stay put, miss. You can't do no good wandering about. My phone went phut away back.'

Lynne patted his shoulder. 'I mean on the doctor's intercom. Do I ask for anyone special?'

Jenkins rubbed his forehead ponderously. 'Tell them to put Tom Driver on—he's a mate of mine. Usually he's on the same shift but his missus was ill and he switched over.' He yawned prodigiously. 'Give me a shake if there's anything you need, miss.'

Feeling more alone than she could remember, Lynne pushed the switch on the intercom and said uncertainly, 'Anyone there? Over.'

The instrument in her hand seemed to quiver with intensity as a high-pitched voice said fervently, 'Thank God you're alive, miss. Can you put the doctor on? Over.'

Lynne forced herself to calmness. 'Dr Layton has been knocked unconscious. I need blankets urgently. Over.'

'Steady on, girl, I'm not exactly Father Christmas! Let me think—if you're in the supply tunnel there should be some emergency equipment. Look for a big box, like a packing case. What about Jenkins? He can tell you. Over.'

It was anger rather than fear that needled Lynne now.

'For your information, Mr Jenkins is trapped—only his arms, shoulders and head are free. Dr Layton gave him morphia before the second roof fall and now he's asleep. Over.'

'Good girl! Now tell us exactly what you can see from where you are—approximately how far you're into the supply tunnel. Take your time. Over.'

The authoritative voice had a calming effect—almost like a ward sister's, Lynne thought absurdly, 'We're about fifty feet inside the supply tunnel. There's a wall of mud blocking the way back, reaching almost to where we are. There've been some more chunks of concrete down since the first fall—the one that trapped Mr Jenkins. That first fall seems to have been mostly from the right side of the supply tunnel. Over.'

'Good girl,' said that distant voice approvingly. 'Now, those emergency supplies should be against the left wall, just about opposite you. Now, swing your lamp on the roof of the tunnel. Any cracks above where you are? Over.'

Lynne's hands trembled as she lifted the heavy lamp. She hadn't had time to think of anything like this. She searched obediently and then put the lamp down carefully. 'There are none directly above us—I haven't looked further on. Over.'

'That's right, stay where you are. The supply tunnel is a dead end, so we'll be getting to you through the mud—can't say how long we'll be—as quick as we can. Anything else? Over.'

Lynne remembered Jenkins' request. 'Mr Jenkins said Mr Tom Driver would know what to do. Over.' Belatedly she decided she could have put it more tactfully.

'You tell Mr Jenkins when he wakes up that Tom Driver has been telling us precisely that ever since the first roof fall. Now, miss, I suggest you look for those emergency supplies and make yourself comfortable until we get to you. Leave the worrying to us. Over and out.'

More easily said than done, Lynne thought crossly as she made her way carefully over to the left side of the tunnel. The operator had been right; the big box was there, partially crushed by a piece of masonry, but Lynne was able to drag out blankets, tearing the polythene covers as she did so. As she searched among the rubble her fingers touched the rough canvas of a knapsack and the bulge of a vacuum flask. One of the men must have put it there just before the accident— perhaps she would find others. But meantime she had some work to do.

Very gently she rolled the Casualty Officer on his side and tucked under a layer of blankets before rolling him back again. Well wrapped in blankets, with a cold compress on his forehead—Lynne had wetted his handkerchief under a convenient water drip—Timothy Layton somehow looked less frightening. His pulse was faint but steady and he showed no signs of regaining consciousness. Lynne left him and made her way back to Jenkins. He appeared to be sleeping peacefully, so Lynne explored the knapsack. The flask was full of hot sweet tea. Carefully Lynne poured herself half a cup and sipped it gratefully. Champagne couldn't have tasted more wonderful.

Just as she was screwing the top of the flask back on, Jenkins opened his eyes. 'Say, miss, I could do with a cuppa.'

For the first time Lynne felt a trifle more cheerful. Helping Jenkins to drink his tea was a little like hospital routine.

'Thanks, miss, that was just the job. How come you brought tea with you?'

Lynne explained.

'Dick Jones must have put it safe for his tea-break. Always one for a cuppa.'

Lynne tucked one of the blankets under his head and round his shoulders. 'How's that, Mr Jenkins?'

'Couldn't have better treatment in hospital, miss. How's the doc?'

Lynne made her way carefully to Timothy Layton's side. It could have been her imagination, but his face seemed to have a greyish tint, though his pulse still beat steadily and was a trifle stronger.

When she got back to Jenkins he was watching her anxiously. 'That lamp's none too clever, miss. Be better if we turned it off for a bit. Saved it for emergencies, if you get what I mean.'

Lynne felt all her old fears bubbling up. 'You mean the battery's going, Mr Jenkins?'

'Put that blanket round you, miss, and sit real close. It won't seem so bad if you can reach out and touch somebody if you get kind of frightened.'

Lynne slowly did as the big man suggested, carefully putting everything within easy reach. With the blanket shutting out some of the clammy chill she began to feel a little warmer. Cautiously she switched off the lamp and the blackness seemed to close down upon her. She tried to control her shudder of terror and then a big hand reached out and held hers comfortingly.

'Seems like you don't care for the dark, miss. There be worse things than darkness—water, for instance, or the black frost. Like to tell me about why you're afraid—of the dark, I mean? You seem pretty brave to me.'

So Lynne told him of the time as a child when she had been locked in a cupboard accidentally during a game of hide and seek and the hideous nightmares she had had for some time afterwards.

'Seems as though you had reason, miss. With the missus it's thunderstorms—she can't abide them. With her she looks for a dark cupboard to hide in, just the opposite to you. She looks a bit like you—same pretty red hair, but she's older and the kids make her tired like. All right now, miss?'

Lynne moved her hand a little within his grasp but she didn't take it away. 'Yes, thank you, Mr Jenkins. Oh, your mate, Tom Driver, is on the rescue job.'

'Then we're as good as out, miss. Tom never gives up.'

In the darkness there was no sense of time. Twice Lynne switched on the lamp and crawled over to Timothy Layton. There was no change, but he didn't seem quite so cold. Carefully she re-wet the compress and replaced it on his forehead, then tucked the blankets back round his shoulders. The only comfort in the situation was that Timothy Layton wasn't conscious to tell what she was doing wrong.

For the first time since Timothy Layton had come to St David's as Senior Casualty Officer there was peace between them. Lynne squatted on her heels and stared down at the unconscious man in the dimming light of the lamp. At thirty-two Timothy Layton had been older than the average holder of the post. Rumour had it that he had only accepted the position because he had failed to get an appointment as a consultant at another hospital. Whether it was disappointment or just his nature, the new Casualty Officer took life very seriously indeed. He hated changed in routine, and Sister Casualty's plans for grooming Lynne for her prospective post hadn't met with his approval. Lynne gave a final glance at the pale face below the shock of dark hair and went back to Jenkins. She would have to think of some way of getting on the good side of Timothy Layton—if he had one.

Jenkins was panting a little as she reached him. 'Better give the blokes a buzz, miss.'

Anxiously she leaned over the big man. 'Is it the pain, Mr Jenkins? I can give you another injection.'

'Not the pain, miss, but the air—it's fouling up!'

For the first time Lynne realised that she was headachy and feeling a little sick. Desperately she fought for calm, and flicked the switch. 'Anyone there? Over.'

A different voice answered this time. 'Something wrong, miss? Over.'

Lynne tried to keep her voice steady. 'It's the air. It's getting foul, Mr Jenkins says. Over.' She could hear a jumble of voices and then:

'Keep your head as near the ground as possible, miss—the air's better there. Don't panic. We'll drive an air pipe through and pump some through to you. We're closer than you think. Over and out.'

Lynne passed the information on to Jenkins, who seemed relieved by the news.

'That makes sense—shouldn't disturb things too much. Doc's all right as he is—couldn't be lower. Pity the rubble didn't knock me over closer to the ground like.'

Lynne touched the big man's shoulder. 'Can I try to shift you, Mr Jenkins?'

The man tried to chuckle. 'You may be from St David's, miss, but not even Goliath could shift this lct!'

Lynne settled down beside him again and switched off the lamp. 'How did you know which hospital I was from?'

'Saw your badge when you and the doc were giving me that injection. We live quite close and the missus takes the kids there and such-like. Save your breath, miss, you're going to need it. If you hears anything switch on the lamp, give them a guide-line to aim for.'

Lynne put one hand on the lamp switch and put her other one on Jenkins' arm. 'Shake me if you want anything, Mr Jenkins. I'm feeling rather sleepy.'

'You have a little nap, miss—won't do you any harm.' His hand slipped over her small one once more. 'Just hang on to me, miss.'

Whether she fell asleep or lost consciousness Lynne could never be sure. She was suddenly aware of a blinding flash of light and someone shouting angrily:

'Get that damn photographer out of here before he blows up the lot of us! Easy there, get the girl on the stretcher and out of here double quick.'

Lynne struggled against the helping hands. 'There's Dr Layton and Mr Jenkins to see to first—I'm all right!'

Someone wrapped her firmly in blankets and lifted her towards the waiting stretcher man. 'Boss's orders, miss. You leave the others to us. Tom Driver's with Jenkins and no one could look after him better. The others have got the doctor. Stop talking, there's a good girl.'

The voice sounded vaguely familiar, but Lynne stopped struggling obediently. She could hear the men carrying the stretcher grunting with the effort as they struggled over the mud, and then blessedly she felt the chill freshness of the air on her face as they emerged into the main tunnel. There was noise and confusion and protesting voices before she was hustled into the friendly security of the St David's ambulance and the scared faces of her two juniors stared down at her. Then the doors slammed and the siren wailed urgently as they gathered speed.

Lynne closed her eyes thankfully, then opened them as one of the juniors tapped her on the shoulder. 'What about Dr Layton? Did he stay behind to look after the trapped men?'

Lynne snorted weakly. 'The great Dr Layton got himself conked on the head and *I've* been looking after him.'

The junior's gasp warned Lynne that perhaps that foul air had dimmed her good judgment, but at that moment the driver opened the sliding window and gazed anxiously in their direction.

'The place is crawling with reporters and TV cameras. How are you feeling, Staff Nurse? It might be safer if I unloaded you at the Nurses' Home and Home Sister can do the necessary.'

Lynne felt suddenly exhausted and close to tears. Reaction, she decided crossly; the sooner she was away from here the better. 'Yes, please, Morgan. I'm all right—just tired.' Her voice quivered a little and she was thankful when the ambulance gathered speed and swayed slightly as the driver turned down a side street.

The two juniors insisted on taking Lynne up to her room. One of them made a pot of tea and the other helped her get into bed.

Home Sister bustled in just as Lynne was sipping the hot tea. 'Oh, here you are, Staff Nurse! Pity no one bothered to inform me. Thank you, Nurses—off you go, and not a word to anyone.' When the door closed behind the juniors, the older woman sat down and looked thoughtfully at Lynne. 'I don't think there's any need for medical attention at the moment. A good night's sleep should do the trick. I'll look in later and the maid can bring you some supper. Anything you want?'

Lynne's lips trembled just a little. 'What about the—others?'

Home Sister looked at her and her expression softened. 'If you mean Dr Layton, he's been admitted to Neuro—severe concussion is the preliminary diagnosis. As for Mr Jenkins, he's in Theatre now—crushed pelvis, they said. Now, you're not to worry—everything possible is being done for them.'

For the first time Lynne remembered her work. 'But I'm supposed to be on duty. What will Casualty Sister think?'

Home Sister stood up. 'That you've had rather a terrible experience and that you're in the right place! I'll be back just before I go off duty.'

The door closed and Lynne saw by the clock on her

dressing table that it was nearly seven o'clock. Five
hours—or very nearly—in that big black hole. It was
only then that Lynne realised that she hadn't been so
terrified after all. Those horrible nightmares belonged to
the past, for always.

It was a commotion outside her door that wakened
Lynne.

'I tell you, I saw it on TV. She was holding hands with
that big chap they brought into Casualty. Very touching,
I call it!'

With a shock Lynne recognised Barbara Stanwell's
voice. She had clashed with the girl ever since she had
come to Casualty as Lynne's junior staff nurse. Lynne
listened more closely, but the nurses must have moved
away.

There was a tap on the door and the maid came in with
a tray. 'Home Sister said to bring you something light,
Staff Nurse. I got you some nice ham and salad from the
staff dining room, ice cream and a piece of cake. Anything else you'd like, you only have to say.'

Lynne sat up and took the tray. 'That's lovely, thank
you, Dorothy. I must have fallen asleep.'

The girl still lingered. 'You must have been ever so
brave. I'd have been scared silly if I'd been trapped like
that. We listened to the reports coming in on the radio—
we didn't know then that it was you and Dr Layton. The
reporters have been hanging round like flies. Matron
was ever so cross, they say.'

Lynne began to feel as if she had awakened to a
strangely confused world. It had never occurred to her
that anyone other than their own casualty team and
possibly the workmen would have been aware of what
had been going on.

'It wasn't really exciting, Dorothy. Thanks for the
tray. I'll leave it outside the door.'

The girl left reluctantly and Lynne heard some whispering and then footsteps going down the corridor.

It was after eight when Home Sister came back. She looked decidedly put out. 'That wretched phone hasn't stopped ringing—I don't know how I'm supposed to do my work with all those interruptions. There's been the doorbell as well, until they put the night porter at the gate.' She glanced approvingly at Lynne's empty tray. 'I'm glad you managed some supper, Staff Nurse. It's a sign that you aren't as affected by your ordeal as those silly young reporters would suggest. That photograph was most unfortunate—not that it was your fault.'

Lynne felt the first touch of unease. 'Could you tell me what's happening, Sister?'

The older woman hesitated and then sat down. 'I keep forgetting that you couldn't possibly know. I don't know all the details, but when the emergency call went out it wasn't long before the papers and the television people got on to it. I don't know whether they were about when you and Dr Layton went into the tunnel—they certainly were when there was the second roof fall. They kept interrupting programmes to bring the latest. They didn't have any names to begin with and as it was a four-ambulance alert I suppose each hospital thought it was one of the others involved until Morgan rang up for instructions. I think one of the reporters must have overheard him or something. Then there was the report about the air supply—' She looked at Lynne thoughtfully. 'It must have been pretty terrible for you. It was very bad management that the photographer got in with the rescue squad. I suppose you had lost consciousness—I don't know.'

'It would help if you told me, Sister,' Lynne pleaded.

'As you'll see it tomorrow anyway, I don't suppose it can do any harm. You must have slumped over the man who was trapped, and you were holding hands, that's all.'

Lynne said simply, 'I've always been terrified of the dark. Mr Jenkins—that's the man who was trapped—knew it, and when we had to turn off the lamp because of the battery he tried to keep me from being frightened, that's all.'

The older woman glanced keenly at Lynne. 'And Dr Layton? What was he doing all this time?'

'He was hit on the head when we first went in, just after he'd given Mr Jenkins the morphia.'

'I see—so in effect there was only you to cope?'

Lynne nodded. 'Yes—and of course the man who answered the intercom; he told me where the blankets were and so on.'

Home Sister patted Lynne's hand. 'Well, try to forget about it, for tonight anyway. I've brought you a mild sedative. I suggest you take it now. I'll see you in the morning.'

'But I have to be on duty,' Lynne protested.

The older woman stood up. 'I'm afraid that won't be possible, my dear. You forget, Casualty is a busy department and can't afford interruptions whatever the reason. Matron will decide what to do.'

Lynne sank back on her pillow in dismay. On the very day she had received the news of her prospective promotion she was both a heroine and an outcast, through no fault of her own, and Dr Timothy Layton was to blame for it all. If only he hadn't insisted on taking her into that big dark hole!

# CHAPTER TWO

HOME Sister's 'mild' sedative was more effective than Lynne had expected. She never heard the morning bell rousing the student nurses. It wasn't until Dorothy shook her into wakefulness and presented her with a breakfast tray and an armful of morning papers that Lynne returned to reality.

'What's all this?' she asked, rubbing her eyes sleepily.

'All about you and the man you helped to rescue, Staff Nurse. You're a proper heroine and no mistake. This is the best photo of you and that Mr Jenkins.' Dorothy thrust one of the newspapers at Lynne.

Lynne's hands shook a little as she spread it out for a better look. For once Home Sister hadn't exaggerated. It looked like something from a 'love-in' or worse. That photographer certainly had an eye for a story!

'Judy saw it on BBC2 and it was in colour. She says it looked smashing, with you and your red hair and the injured chap with his fair hair, and the pair of you holding hands for dear life.'

A tap on the door sent Dorothy to a hasty exit as Home Sister came in.

She frowned when she saw the array of papers. 'Dorothy, I suppose. I'd better have a word with her. Next thing we know she'll be offering your life story to one of the Sunday papers! This place has been like a madhouse this morning. One of the porters caught a cameraman on the fire escape—a good thing you have a corner room. Matron wants to see you at ten o'clock. If you make a point of going over with the girls going on duty then, you should pass unnoticed, we hope. At least you aren't the only redhead at St David's. Did you sleep well?'

Lynne nodded. 'Yes, thank you. Your sedative did the trick, Sister.' She hesitated. 'Is Matron very annoyed?'

'Well, you could say that this unwanted publicity has given Admin. a lot of extra work.' She sighed. 'A pity no one warned Mr Jenkins to keep quiet—I suppose the morphia made him talkative. The reporters not only got to him in Casualty but someone got past the night nurse—I can't think what St David's is coming to! Now, for goodness' sake, be careful what you say to *anyone*!'

Home Sister was gone before Lynne could ask any more questions. She ate her cooling breakfast with little appetite. Yesterday morning had been such a red letter one, but this one looked like being a worse ordeal than what she had gone through in that wretched tunnel.

At five to ten Lynne joined the procession of nurses going on duty. Fortunately it was raining and everyone was so preoccupied with getting to the hospital block without spoiling the crispness of their uniforms that Lynne escaped with only a few teasing remarks. As she rounded the corner to Matron's office she almost bumped into Barbara Stanwell, Casualty junior staff nurse. The girl made no response to Lynne's hasty apology but merely stared at her with such an air of malicious triumph that Lynne felt uneasy. So far the relations between them had been slightly strained simply because Lynne objected to the girl's wasting so much time flirting madly with any man who appeared in Casualty, from junior reporters to senior consultants. Lynne had overheard the juniors scathingly refer to the younger girl as Bibs—they said she positively drooled over anything in trousers.

Matron's light flashed on as Lynne knocked. She went in and stood stiffly in front of the desk. 'You wished to see me, Matron.'

'Yes, Staff Nurse. Please sit down. Home Sister reports that you appear to have recovered from your ordeal yesterday. It is a very unfortunate business, and I have just heard something exceedingly disquieting. Perhaps you would be kind enough to tell me precisely why you went with the emergency team yesterday when you hadn't even reported back for duty?'

Lynne was thankful for the chair underneath her. The unexpectedness of the attack left her shaking. 'Because Dr Layton insisted, Matron.' She couldn't very well explain the method of her inclusion—her pride still smarted from the indignity of being hoisted aboard the ambulance.

Matron was plainly surprised. 'I was not aware that Dr Layton was in charge of Casualty's nursing staff,' she retorted icily. 'In fact no one knew you were with the team until Morgan reported for instructions hours later. You might be interested to learn that Sister Casualty had to give up her off-duty on your account.' Matron tapped her desk in irritation and for the first time Lynne saw the pile of newspaper cuttings. 'Leaving that point for the moment, I am at a loss to understand why you went into the tunnel with Dr Layton. It certainly isn't routine for our nurses to do so. It would have been far more suitable for the medical students to have gone.'

Lynne fought for calmness. 'Dr Layton told me to come with him, Matron. He said he needed my assistance—' Her voice trailed off. It all sounded unconvincing.

'To help him give a simple injection of morphia? Really, Staff Nurse, a medical student could have managed that!'

Lynne tried again. 'Dr Layton did ask me to bring the small drum—the amputation drum,' she added miserably.

'I am well aware of what the small drum contains, Staff Nurse! Since Dr Layton hasn't recovered consciousness yet it isn't possible to check with him why he departed from routine procedure. The impression I've been given is that you've managed to thrust yourself forward in a most unfortunate way. The question of whether it was deliberate or not is still unresolved.'

Lynne could stand no more. 'But, Matron, I would *never*, never have gone into that dark hole without a direct order!' She covered her face with her hands, her whole body shaking with great shudders.

Matron got to her feet and came round the desk. 'Pull yourself together, Staff Nurse.' Her voice softened a little and her hand rested on Lynne's shoulder. 'Are you trying to tell me that you suffer from claustrophobia?'

Lynne nodded and mopped her eyes apologetically. 'I was accidentally locked in a dark cupboard when I was small—'

'I see. That could have made things much more of an ordeal for you, but it doesn't quite explain everything.' She went back to her seat. 'I think that in the circumstances it would be better if you had a couple of days off. Then you can finish off the week on the night shift. That should give the reporters time to find another story.'

Lynne sat there numbly. She was being sent home in disgrace; she was being put on the night shift—a junior's job. 'But what about—?' but she couldn't get the words out. It didn't seem like the right moment to ask if her promotion still stood.

'Naturally you're upset, Staff Nurse. You'll see that it's all for the best in a day or two. I'll phone Home

Sister—she can help you with any arrangements you have to make.'

Lynne stood up, not trusting herself to more than a brief, 'Thank you, Matron.'

She emerged into the corridor again and started back in the direction of the Nurses' Home, like a sleepwalker neither knowing nor caring what she was doing. Someone grabbed her by the arm and without looking up she struggled to free herself.

'Steady on, Lynne, it's only your safe old Uncle Ben checking up on you.' Ben Gresham's tone altered. 'What on earth's the matter, Lynne? Has the She-Dragon been grilling you on both sides? Bet old St Lawrence couldn't have looked worse than you!' He took Lynne firmly by the arm. 'We're having a coffee in the canteen forthwith. None of our crowd will be there this early and the department can do without its Junior Casualty Officer for ten minutes. Most people are fighting shy of us at the moment—they prefer to have their cuts and bruises patched up, without publicity.' He saw Lynne wince and went on hastily, 'I've booked a nice juicy murder for three o'clock. By the time the newshawks discover it's a false alarm they won't bother coming back here! Sit down.'

Lynne sat down thankfully. She hadn't realised how tightly wound up she was until the rush of Ben Gresham's chatter had washed over her. He came back with two cups of coffee and two large jam doughnuts.

'Not another word until you've got yours down to the last drop and crumb. Meanwhile I'll fill you in. First, dear Bibs turns up in Casualty all smiles and no claws showing. I asked after you, real casual-like, and she did the great transformation scene and stalked off muttering that she'd cooked your goose good and proper. I went all coy and eager and followed her, but all I could cadge out of her was a few hints that you and old Timothy needn't try to play the innocent.'

Lynne put down her cup with a clatter. 'Does Barbara think she should have gone with the emergency squad yesterday?' she demanded.

'Well, as a matter of fact I think she and I should have gone. We were the ones on duty at that precise moment.'

Lynne stared at him. 'Then why didn't you?'

Ben looked sheepish. 'We weren't exactly available,' he admitted. 'We were having a little heart-to-heart in the linen cupboard and by the time we realised what all the commotion was about, old Timothy was doing the big hero act and kidnapping you as he went past.'

'You mean you actually saw Dr Layton grab me?'

'I did. I was at the window by that time—I don't know about dear Bibs. She was doing a quickstep to greet Sister Casualty coming back from lunch. I decided that I had urgent business elsewhere and went out the back way.'

'Matron said that no one knew where I was until Morgan phoned back,' Lynne said slowly.

Ben gave her a quick glance. 'I wouldn't know about that, Lynne, old girl. I suppose it never occured to me that people didn't know. All I was concerned about was not to be around when Timothy came back. His temper can be tricky, but this time it was pretty foul. He was in Sister Casualty's office holding forth—she was late going to lunch—and he was muttering all over the place. That was why I made myself scarce in the first place. Then when we didn't hear the emergency call! The Fifth of November will seem pretty tame by comparison! Luckily you saved my bacon—I'm only sorry you got yours grilled in return.'

'Thanks for your sympathy!' Lynne said tartly. 'At least you can confirm that I didn't snatch Barbara Stanwell's chance for glory from choice!'

'Steady on, Lynne! I can't confirm any story without dropping at least two people on the old gridiron, and as one of those is myself, you can count me out! Let Timothy Layton pull the chestnuts out—after all, he's the one who involved you, not me.'

'He's still unconscious, Ben, and Matron's putting me on nights for the rest of the week, from Thursday night,' Lynne explained miserably.

But Ben only chuckled. 'Cheer up, little maiden. Uncle Ben will keep you company. With Timothy out of the running I'll be well tied down. I'll pass the word out that we don't want casualties faster than one per hour until further notice. That will just give us time for coffee and sandwiches and pleasant chats between cases.'

'Ben, please be serious for one moment!' Lynne pleaded, knowing that the big fair-haired Junior Casualty Officer would only treat it as another glorious joke. To him even tragedy had its funny side.

'Not another word, Lynne. Keep that little frilly cap on the back of your head and all will work out. Oh, by the way, that big chap you were canoodling with in the tunnel has been asking for you. I think he wants to hold your hand some more!' He dodged the blow Lynne threatened him with and got to his feet. 'That's better! Smile—it suits you better. You're as bad as Timothy Layton, you take life too seriously! Well, I'll be off. See you Thursday night. Meanwhile I'll snuggle up to dear Bibs and see what's on the agenda for her claws!'

The canteen seemed strangely silent after Ben Gresham's departure. Lynne hastily finished her coffee and doughnut and found they went down better than she had expected. Ben's foolery had done her more good than she realised. Perhaps she did take life too seriously.

Home Sister greeted Lynne on her return. 'Your aunt

has been on the phone. She's collecting you at half-past twelve. It seems that your parents think it will be more of a rest for you there.' She saw Lynne's expression. 'Yes, they've had reporters as well. Never mind, Staff Nurse, by this time next week you'll be "Bottom of the Pops".'

'But life will never be the same!' Lynne burst out.

'You'll be surprised to discover just how similar it can be,' the older woman said dryly. 'Do you want a couple of sedative tablets to take with you?'

Lynne shook her head. 'No, thanks, Sister—if I'm to get back to normal.'

Home Sister smiled. 'Get yourself packed, my dear. I've told your aunt to park by the garden entrance, so if you go out that way—and wear a head-scarf, there's a good girl!'

Lynne tucked in a stray curl and surveyed her reflection in the mirror. With the dark blue scarf hiding her red curls, black shadows under her hazel eyes emphasising her pallor, there was little resemblance to the Staff Nurse Lynne Howard who had gone lightheartedly back on duty yesterday. It would take a reporter with radar eyes to find her right now.

Lynne's Aunt Jenny greeted her with concern. 'Get in, child. I don't think they've suspected me as yet. I saw one or two cameramen as I came past the main entrance. You look as if you were buried for five days, not five hours! What on earth possessed you to go in that tunnel? You were always scared silly by the dark.'

Lynne huddled down in her seat. 'I know, Aunt Jenny, but as a nurse you have to do what you're told.' She grabbed for a hold as her aunt swung suddenly down a side street.

'That wretched man, jumping out like that! I don't think he saw you, dear—just checking, I suppose. Anyway, your parents will be joining us for dinner tonight at the Cambrian. They'll never look for you there—too dull, but at least the food's good. I'm sure the change will work wonders.'

It was such a relief to be swallowed up into the quiet comfort of Jenny Leslie's flat. She was Lynne's godmother, but she had always been called Aunt Jenny, and Lynne knew she wouldn't be bothered by questions unless she wanted to answer them.

After lunch Lynne was settled by the fire, surrounded by magazines and books, soothed by the beauty of the bowls of autumn flowers, and left to relax on her own.

'I'll be back at teatime. The cleaning woman will be doing upstairs, but she has her own key, so you won't be disturbed if you happen to doze off.'

There was soft music on the radio and the fire was warm and cosy. Lynne put her magazine down and leaned back with her eyes closed. The peacefulness was so wonderful that it almost hurt.

She was roused abruptly by a sharp clattering noise and an exclamation of astonishment.

'So you're the one! I never thought it'd be you!'

Lynne opened her eyes to see a strange woman in a green overall standing over her. It took her a few seconds to realise that this must be Aunt Jenny's cleaning woman, but what was she talking about?

'I just came in to make up the fire as I always do. Mrs Leslie mentioned she had a visitor, but I never guessed. My Ron was on and on about you when they let me see him. He kept saying something about red hair.' There was a soft unexpected chuckle. 'Fancy us meeting like this!'

Lynne sat up. 'You're Mrs Jenkins, then. I remember your husband saying you lived near St David's—and that you had pretty red hair,' she added shyly.

The cleaning woman laughed. 'Bet he hasn't noticed it

in years! Must have been something terrible in that tunnel. Ron said you were ever so brave—not a tear or a scream out of you. Can't think why that doctor fellow took a young thing like you with him, though come to think of it there'd have been no one to tell Tom Driver where you all were after the doctor copped one. I'm ever so grateful to you, Nurse, and so glad I found you. I tried Outpatients before I came away, but a real snippy nurse told me you weren't working there now—wore a red belt, she did.'

Lynne stifled a sigh. Barbara Stanwell must be putting in overtime on her hate programme. 'I've got a couple of days off,' she explained. 'Could you give my best wishes to your husband when you see him tonight? And please say thanks to him for me, Mrs Jenkins.'

'Thank my Ron? Whatever next?'

'He kept me from being frightened of the dark,' Lynne said simply. 'How is he going on?'

'Fractured pelvis and badly bruised,' Mrs Jenkins said promptly. 'The doctor says he'll go on all right, barring complications. You should see the telegrams and flowers and stuff he's had—some of it from people he never even heard of. Well, I must be off, Nurse.' She started towards the door and then turned back. 'I expect you're busy, Nurse, but if you have a moment to look in on my Ron, I know he'd be ever so pleased.'

For the first time Lynne could look back on yesterday afternoon with a warm feeling of satisfaction. At least some good had come out of all that horror.

Aunt Jenny came bustling in with the tea tray before Lynne had time to wonder how long she had been sleeping.

She greeted Lynne cheerfully. 'Well, no one appears to have followed you here. Perhaps they've taken off the heat by now.'

'It was your Mrs Jenkins' husband who was trapped, that they took the photograph of with me!' Lynne burst out incoherently.

Mrs Leslie whistled. 'I should have thought of that. I remember she did tell me her husband drove one of those ditch-diggers. I hope she won't talk.'

'I don't think so, except to her Ron,' Lynne said softly. 'He's going to be all right—they've told her so.'

'Well, I hope it wasn't just some soft soap. Oh, by the way, they found the other three men. No, not dead. They'd slipped away to place a bet on a horse they fancied. I don't suppose your Mr Jenkins even knew, or else he covered up for them—before things happened, I mean.'

'So that was why he didn't sound concerned when I found the knapsack with the flask of tea.' Lynne was relieved to find that she could talk quite normally about what had happened. She made no reference to her conversation with Matron this morning—that was hospital business, and Aunt Jenny might just mention it to her parents.

The dinner with her parents went off far better than Lynne had anticipated. Aunt Jenny kept the conversation on a light note and the Howards seemed satisfied that their daughter had come to no harm.

'It's as bad as having a pop star in the family,' her father teased her. 'The questions those reporters asked us—your mother is still blushing! However, I think I'd better have a word with Matron. I don't think you should have been allowed to go into such a dangerous place.'

'Please, Dad, leave it for now. There's been enough bother already and Matron is looking into the matter,' Lynne begged.

'All right, dear, we'll leave it for the moment. It's just that we know how you feel about—'

'I'm not afraid of the dark any more, Mother,' Lynne broke in. 'Mr Jenkins helped me to get over it.'

Her parents exchanged a look. 'That's something to be thankful for at any rate. How about the doctor? I suppose you had two patients to look after instead of just the one.'

Lynne nodded. 'Not that there was much that I could do for them. Dr Layton is still unconscious as far as I know.'

Her mother shivered. 'To think it could have been you!'

Mr Howard touched his wife on the shoulder. 'Well, it wasn't, Anne. I'll just settle the bill and make sure the coast is clear. We'd better go out separately, just in case.'

Lynne began to feel more like a near-criminal than a near-heroine. It was all so ridiculous. The only good thing was that no one had been killed, and at least she hadn't been the one to knock Timothy Layton over the head. If only there weren't all the complications at work! Perhaps Ben Gresham would have sorted things out by Thursday night.

As Aunt Jenny turned into the drive someone got out of a car parked across the road and came towards them. Lynne shrank down into the shadow, but as the figure came under the street lamp she realised that it was Ben Gresham. Her heart sank. There must be some serious complications for him to come looking for her at this hour.

'Sorry, Mrs Leslie, to intrude upon you at this hour, but it's rather urgent.'

'Hadn't you better come into the house and explain your problem?' Mrs Leslie suggested.

'I'm afraid there isn't time—I had to leave a house surgeon standing in for me.' He looked at Lynne appealingly. 'I know it will sound funny coming from me, but Timothy Layton has regained consciousness and he sent me to fetch you. He's getting all worked up about something—says he can't settle down unless I bring you forthwith. I tried to explain that I didn't know where you were, but he wouldn't buy it.'

'How did you find us, young man?' Mrs Leslie asked suspiciously.

'Buttered up Home Sister and convinced her that my heart would break unless I could see you tonight,' Ben answered shamelessly.

They had to laugh. It was Lynne who made the decision.

'All right, Ben, I'll come, but it must be on the quiet.'

Mrs Leslie was horrified. 'You mean this isn't through official channels?'

Ben shrugged his shoulders. 'It would take too long, and time's short. I'll have Lynne back within the hour, that's a promise.'

'I don't like the sound of it, but since Lynne agrees, I don't suppose I have the authority to forbid it. For goodness' sake be careful.'

Lynne followed Ben into his car reluctantly. 'Is this on the level, Ben, or just one of your mad schemes?'

'Don't be so darned suspicious, girl! Do you think I'd do this for a man I dislike unless it was really urgent?'

Lynne had to be satisfied with that, although her every instinct shouted beware!

As she followed Ben up the fire stairs that led to the Neurological Block Lynne felt even more uneasy. This was crazy, and if Matron heard about it—well, she'd have to emigrate or something.

Ben put a hand on her arm and whispered: 'Wait here, Lynne, while I check on all the odd bods. Won't be long.'

The heavy fire door thudded dully behind him and Lynne waited in the semi-darkness for his return. Ben was back before she had time to change her mind.

'It's all right. Night Sister has done her round and Staff Nurse has gone to supper. There's only a junior at this end and she's with young Carey—head injuries on quarter-hourly P.R. and B.P. Timothy Layton's in the side ward on the left. I'll collect you in half an hour.'

Lynne caught at Ben's jacket. 'You mean I'm to go in on my own?'

'That's right—Dr Layton's orders, to be precise. Stop worrying, girl. He's senior enough to carry any cans.' He gave her a gentle push. 'On the left. No need to knock—you're expected.'

Expected or not, Lynne's push on the door of the side ward was very timid indeed. Feeling like a conspirator, she slipped quickly in and closed it behind her. She leanded against the panels and gazed shyly in the direction of the bed. She had forgotten how tall Timothy Layton was, and he seemed to overflow the spartan narrowness of the hospital bed. The bruise over his temple was beginning to change from black to a greenish-orange. The dark hair, now neatly brushed once more, showed up the same pallor that had worried her yesterday.

Timothy Layton had moved his head cautiously at the sound of her entry. 'Sit down, Staff Nurse, in that chair where I can see you without lifting my head. Whew! I've got the grandfather of a headache, and that light doesn't help. Can you move it a little? You were very good to come like this.'

Lynne obeyed his instructions cautiously. This was the second time in two days that she wasn't consciously afraid of the Senior Casualty Officer, but she couldn't help feeling that she must be ready to jump if he lashed out at her with one of his sarcastic remarks.

'I had to be sure that you were really all right, Staff Nurse, and that they weren't just making soothing remarks to soothe an injured man. It was all my fault you were trapped in that tunnel. You shouldn't have been there at all. I don't know quite how to apologise—'

'That's all right, Dr Layton. I didn't come to any harm, and I was able to help a little.' She stopped, feeling that he might think she was boasting about her part. Then curiosity took over. 'What did you mean by saying I shouldn't have been there?'

'The juniors told me you weren't on duty, but I couldn't find that other staff nurse and the matter was urgent. I didn't stop to think when I saw you coming. I'm not much good at explaining things when I'm in a hurry. Besides, there was another reason.'

To her amazement Lynne saw a slight flush of colour creeping over Timothy Layton's pale face. 'What was it?' Somehow it didn't seem to be strange to put such a question.

'Sounds silly, I know, but as you always seemed so tidy and efficient I wanted to know how you would cope with an emergency like the tunnel.'

It *did* sound silly, and so unlike the deadly serious Dr Timothy Layton that Lynne began to wonder if the blow on the head had affected his cool common sense. Then to her horror she heard footsteps coming along the corridor, and they certainly weren't Ben's rather ponderous ones.

Dr Layton saw her alarm. 'Pull your chair closer to the bed and leave this to me,' he hissed fiercely.

The door behind Lynne's back opened slowly and she had to resist the urge to turn and look.

'Oh, I didn't know you had a visitor, Dr Layton. I'm sure Night Sister wouldn't approve if—'

'My fiancée is just leaving, Nurse Saxton. I wouldn't mind a cup of tea if you're making one,' Timothy Layton said smoothly.

'I'll be back in five minutes, Dr Layton,' and then the door closed softly.

Lynne didn't know which way to look, and then she saw that Timothy Layton was watching her quizzically.

'There's no need to appear so shocked, Staff Nurse. I assure you that I only said it to get rid of the wretched girl. It doesn't involve you in any way at all.'

At the hint of sarcasm colouring his voice Lynne flinched. 'I wasn't thinking of that. It was just that—'

'You never thought me human enough to think up such an excuse, eh? Never mind, Staff Nurse. Run along, and thank you for coming. You can leave me to my headache and to my misery—not that it will bring those three lives back!'

Lynne paused and then instinctively bent over Timothy Layton reassuringly. 'No one was killed, Dr Layton! The three men had taken some unofficial time off, that's all. And as for Ron Jenkins, I've been talking to his wife and she says he's going to be all right.'

To her alarm and astonishment Lynne saw slow tears roll down Timothy Layton's cheeks. Tactfully she turned away and tiptoed out of the room. This time it was Ben Gresham coming along the corridor, and Lynne was too full of her own thoughts to notice that Ben, too, had something on his mind.

There was nothing but quiet streets and silence within the car as Ben drove her back to Aunt Jenny's. He stopped the car under the street light and waited for Lynne to get out.

'Thank you for the lift, Ben,' she said absently.

'You might have told Uncle Ben about it.' Ben's tone was faintly accusing.

'About what?' Lynne drew her hand back from the door handle.

'About being old Timothy's fiancée.'

Lynne stared and then smiled a little. 'Oh, that—I thought you knew all about situations like that. Good night, Ben, and thanks.'

She got out of the car and walked through the gate, not really noticing—or caring—that she had left a badly puzzled young man behind her.

# CHAPTER THREE

LYNNE found Aunt Jenny sitting in her housecoat by the fire. The older woman glanced at her goddaughter with some anxiety.

'Thank goodness you're back! I had visions of trying to explain your absence—let alone the reasons for it—to your parents. Is this Dr Layton all right? I think it quite ridiculous that he should have asked for you at this hour, especially after we've tried so hard to keep you away from those wretched reporters!'

Lynne sat down hastily. 'I'm sorry, Aunt Jenny. I didn't want to go, but I'm glad I did.' Her face wore the same dreamy look that had puzzled Ben Gresham.

Mrs Leslie looked at the girl sharply. 'Don't you think you'd better tell me what happened?'

Lynne nodded. 'Not that there's much to tell. Dr Layton was worrying himself sick. Oh, I don't mean about me—at least not specially. He thought the other men had been killed, apart from Ron Jenkins. He was upset because he thought he had failed—as if he could have stopped that rock hitting him!' Lynne sat very still for a moment. 'Do you know, Aunt Jenny, he actually cried when I told him they were safe. And I always thought he was so tough and hard-hearted and un-reasonable. I have been silly,' she added almost to herself as if she had forgotten the older woman's presence.

Mrs Leslie coughed gently. 'I expect he's still suffering from concussion or whatever you have after a blow on the head. I've left everything ready for a cup of chocolate if you'd like to go through and make it. There's cake in the tin if you're hungry. I thought you might be bringing that young man back with you—Dr Gresham.'

Lynne got to her feet. 'He had to go back on duty, if you remember. Someone was standing in for him.'

'What did he think of your tough man's tears?'

Lynne gave her godmother a startled glance. 'Ben? He wasn't there. He had to stand guard.' She hurried off to the kitchen. Perhaps it hadn't been quite such a good idea telling someone else, even someone as understanding as her godmother. It was just that it had all been so unexpected—especially Timothy Layton's remedy for getting rid of the junior night nurse. If only Ben hadn't found out—he had a forgetful way of not keeping secrets.

The next morning was one of those golden mornings that made winter seem very far away. Lynne and her godmother took the car and a packed lunch and drove through the bright glow of an autumn countryside.

'Forget St David's even exists,' Jenny Leslie told Lynne firmly. 'What a pity you're tied to a job. We could pack our bags and tour the Continent.'

'But I haven't got any money,' Lynne objected sadly. 'In any case I like my job and my prospects even better.' Then she remembered the threat to those very prospects.

'You sound forty-three and not twenty-three,' her godmother suggested dryly. 'However, we agreed not to talk about St David's—or haven't you any life outside those grey walls?'

Lynne flushed. Even playful little games seemed to develop sharp corners. 'Some. I still go to the youth club and I belong to a record group.'

'Pop, I suppose.' Mrs Leslie laughed ruefully. 'I keep

forgetting the age gap. It isn't the years, it's the language.'

'Only the best of pops,' Lynne insisted. 'We collect other stuff as well. But lately I haven't had so much time. We've been short-handed in Casualty and I've had to work late.'

'And all paths end up right back to St David's! Like to go on the river? I don't think it will be too cool. There isn't any wind and we can always find a sunny corner to tie up for lunch. Canoe or punt?'

Lynne hesitated. 'Punt, I think. It's more comfortable.'

'Well said, provided you weren't trying to cushion my extra ten years.' Mrs Leslie found a parking place and let Lynne carry the picnic basket.

As it was mid-week the river wasn't crowded and once Lynne had pushed the punt well away from the landing place they seemed to be in a land worlds away from the bustle of St David's. Moorhens ran away over the reed beds as they approached and a water-vole hastily changed his direction when they came too close. A cheeky water-rat sat in the sun and preened his whiskers and didn't even deign to move away. Two swans paddled strongly up and turned away with disappointed hissings when no food was forthcoming.

Jenny Leslie trailed her fingers in the water. 'If only these golden days could be all the year round I wouldn't mind a cottage by the river. I remember when John and I—' She stopped suddenly and seemed to be studying some object on the bank.

Lynne kept a tactful silence. She had never been actually told what had happened to John Leslie—whether he had died, been divorced, or simply gone away. She supposed her parents knew, but she had never asked. Her godmother seemed to have enough money to live on comfortably, although she did do research work for various authors from time to time. Lynne supposed it must bring in some income, or perhaps Jenny Leslie simply did it for something to fill in the length of the days.

'Head for that sunny corner, Lynne. I don't think the swans will bother us there.'

Lynne obeyed. Someone must have been cutting the reeds on this stretch leaving a series of notches each just big enough to take a punt and leaving a tactful curtain of reeds between each notch.

A faint fitful breeze sang through the reeds like fairy music and occasionally a small rustle suggested that some tiny unseen bird or beast was making its way through the tall stems. Lynne and her godmother ate their sandwiches in a comfortable sort of silence. The momentary embarrassment that had followed the older woman's unfinished sentence seemed to have vanished.

Jenny Leslie drained her cup of coffee. 'Every city-dweller should spend a day like this at least once a fortnight.' She stretched herself lazily. 'It would take out all the kinks. Tell me more about Ben Gresham—he certainly seems to have plenty of go about him. Are you going steady, or whatever the current term is?'

Lynne chuckled. 'No one could go steady with Ben Gresham! The more the merrier goes as far as he's concerned. I like him, but so do a lot of other girls. He's good fun and as cheeky as they come, but no one takes him seriously—not if they have any sense.'

'But he's old enough to think about settling down, surely?'

'A twenty-six-year-old Junior Casualty Officer with any serious ambitions won't be thinking about settling down for at least another six years. He won't have the money, for one thing, and he's got to be free to move round at a moment's notice. If he's married and his wife isn't a doctor and they have one or two kids he can be a G.P. or emigrate—there's no other future unless they win the pools or have a wealthy relative. It just isn't on.'

'What about your Dr Layton, then?' Jenny Leslie asked idly. 'I take it he's older.'

Lynne wondered at the unexpected question, but answered readily enough. 'About six years, but they say he missed the boat—I mean he didn't get the consultant's post he was after. It wasn't at St David's, so I don't really know.'

'Is he married?'

Lynne stared at her godmother, but the older woman's eyes were half closed against the brightness of the sun and her expression betrayed no particular emotion.

'To be perfectly honest we don't know, and he's not the kind you ask that sort of question over elevenses. He's only been at St David's a few months. He didn't come with the half-yearly turnover, so he escaped the usual quizzing.'

'What off-duty interests has this dark horse got, or don't you know?'

Lynne had to chuckle. 'Talk about a third degree! He gives lectures on safety to schoolchildren at the schools and I think he gives talks on the same subject to the parents—and someone did say they'd seen his name down on a WI programme.'

'Sounds rather stuffy and a bit of an old woman to me.' Jenny Leslie yawned frankly. 'Take my advice and don't get involved with Dr Layton—you'll lead a very dull life. I'm going to have twenty winks.'

Lynne's instinctive leap to defend Dr Timothy Layton

subsided abruptly, especially as she realised that here she had been about to speak up for the man with whom she had been on sparring terms ever since he had turned up in Casualty. She snuggled down on the punt cushions and found herself remembering those slow tears rolling down Timothy Layton's cheeks.

She must have dozed off when a sudden blast from a transistor roused her abruptly. She hadn't heard a punt go by. It sounded almost on top of them, the blare from the hidden radio and outbursts of laughter and high-pitched voices trying to outdo the shrill music. Lynne did little more than register annoyance until one unseen speaker's words coincided with a musical pause.

'—I'm telling you that Bibs swears she saw Howard coming from the Neuro block. Listen, Janie, I know she's supposed to be off sick—delayed shock and all that—but according to dear Bibs it's all a put-up thing until the heat dies down. You're wrong. Howard's all right—just old-fashioned—'

The music flared up again and drowned any further conversation. Lynne lay back against her cushions again, trembling with anger. Of course she had been a junior once and quite as outspoken against her seniors, but it was different when it was overheard, and it hurt—horribly. She hadn't been able to identify the speaker. The river was too popular a place with St David's staff to make any detective work possible. In any case it would be embarrassing enough wondering who thought she was stuffy without actually knowing.

A sudden movement of the punt made Lynne sit up. To her astonishment Aunt Jenny was poking the punt paddle furtively into the reeds. Lynne peered more closely just as the older woman lifted it triumphantly and Lynne saw a length of rope slither across the wide blade and slide through the rushes.

Jenny Leslie turned and saw Lynne watching her and put her finger to her lips. The two women waited for several minutes and then it was apparent that the music from the transistor was getting fainter.

There was a sudden shout. 'Janie! You silly idiot—I thought you knew how to tie a boat up!'

Lynne's godmother chuckled. 'That'll learn them! They'll have a nice long paddle back from the weir pool.'

'You heard then?' Lynne's cheeks felt uncomfortably warm.

'Well, you certainly can't sue anyone for slander on the basis of that! In any case, being old-fashioned is quite refreshing these days, my dear, so don't let it throw you. I take it that this Bibs person is that junior staff nurse who's always getting your ruffles up?'

Lynne nodded. 'Yes. Oh, Barbara Stanwell is efficient enough, but she's so silly with it, always flirting and drawing attention to herself.'

'I suppose that Ben Gresham is one of those she flirts with. Can I detect just a little jealousy here?'

Lynne flushed again. 'Ben's only a good friend. I told you, he's not the serious kind, Aunt Jenny.'

'But that doesn't prevent the girls from getting serious. Perhaps this girl really does care and is simply trying to cover up the fact.'

Lynne sighed. 'Then it's a funny way of doing it. She certainly fooled me. Shall I start paddling back now?'

The older woman nodded. 'Might as well. The sun's distinctly reminded us that it's September. I wish I'd known those wretched girls were going to spoil our outing.'

Lynne hastened to reassure her. 'It's all right, Aunt Jenny. I never thought of it either. As juniors our set always headed for the river—it was cheaper than window-shopping and less frustrating. We would pool our shillings and save up our biscuits from elevenses. I suppose it was something like what you said—escape from the city and—'

'—all the pain and suffering you nurses put up with every day. I couldn't do it. I'd be like your Timothy Layton and weep over it. Only I'd keep on crying my eyes out until they let me go.'

'It's not like that all the time, and we get used to it. I don't mean hard-boiled, but able to keep our feelings under control—at least most of the time. I admit Casualty can be heartbreaking, especially when they bring in kids knocked down in traffic—'

'Stop it, Lynne! This is supposed to be a day off,' Jenny Leslie reminded her firmly.

'Sorry, but when it's most of your life it's like trying to pull out threads, and you can't without spoiling the pattern. Anyway, thanks for trying. It's been a lovely day in spite of—the interruptions.'

Thursday afternoon found Lynne trying to sleep—not that it would do much good. There were no short cuts to the first night on night duty. She knew she would feel like death by about two a.m.—shivering with cold even on a warm night and with eyelids too heavy for matchsticks to keep open, a little sick and with muscles that shouted for sleep. Perhaps it would be a busy night and she wouldn't have a moment to think about how she felt. She remembered Ben Gresham's absurd promise to watch out the night with her. Of course the ward would keep him busy—intravenous drips needing attention, emergency admissions, cases for theatre. Casualty only had first call, that was all, and she couldn't see Ben Gresham wasting time on a girl too sleepy to appreciate his company. For one silly moment Lynne wished she could be as casual and light-hearted as Barbara Stanwell.

Lynne left her godmother's with just enough time to change into uniform before going on duty. She wanted to avoid the curious glances and the spate of questions. She only hoped that Sister Casualty would be on duty for the hand-over. The older woman normally went off at five, but with Lynne away there would have had to be some changes in the rota unless Matron had lent another staff nurse to the department.

It was raining slightly and there was a nasty wind whipping at the ends of the nurses' cloaks and trying to snatch off their caps. No one seemed to notice Lynne as she turned off the main corridor for Casualty. All the trolleys and wheelchairs were neatly lined up outside the swing doors and only the side lights were on in the main waiting hall, so Lynne guessed that there were no cases being dealt with. She would be on her own until the junior float finished helping on the wards at ten o'clock—unless of course more than one casualty came in.

To Lynne's relief it was Sister Casualty sitting behind the desk when she went into the office. To her over-strained senses the older woman seemed unusually quiet, but perhaps it was simply weariness. She gave the report in her usual concise manner and handed Lynne the keys.

'It's not our take-in night, so unless there are some accidents on the doorstep you should have a peaceful night. We could do with some extra dressings and perhaps you would check the plaster room—we had a run of fractures today. You would have thought it was icy November. I think that's all, Staff Nurse.' She got to her feet and came round the desk. 'I'm glad you're safely back, Staff Nurse.' She gave Lynne an awkward little pat on the shoulder and walked stiffly towards the door.

For once Lynne was too taken aback to escort her senior off the premises. There were still a thousand questions unanswered, but at least Sister Casualty hadn't altered her attitude—at least not completely. With that she would have to be content. The excitement of Monday's promotion-to-be was now a faraway memory and she would have to tread softly until the episode of the tunnel and that wretched photograph was smothered under the rush of casualties.

Lynne waited until the last echo of Sister Casualty's footsteps had died away before she went on a slow tour of inspection. She hadn't done night duty in Casualty since she had been a senior student, and *that* seemed years ago. Of course the routine procedures were the same at night, but it meant she would have to cope with the emergency on her own until the night casualty team assembled from their various duty points.

Lynne was checking the supplies in the tiny kitchen which served the department when she heard hurrying footsteps coming across the main waiting hall.

'Hsst! Lynne, where have you got yourself to?'

Lynne came to the door warily, then relaxed when she saw that it was Ben Gresham. 'A little more respect, Dr Gresham, if you please!' she said severely.

'Don't be so stuffy, Lynne—there's no one about, and you can't tell me these walls have ears.'

Lynne winced a little—to be called stuffy twice in just over twenty-four hours was a bit much. 'I know, Ben. It's just that—'

'You've had a rough time and the powers-that-be haven't exactly treated you like a heroine.' He put a comforting arm round her shoulders, and Lynne discovered to her astonishment that she wasn't in her usual hurry to withdraw.

She dabbed furtively at her eyes. 'I'm just being silly,'

she admitted. 'Thanks, Ben. Is there a case on its way?'

'When it's not our take-in? Not as long as Uncle Ben is on call. Can't you believe that I simply wanted to see that you were all right? After all, I did promise.'

Lynne gently released herself. 'Thanks, Ben. I do appreciate it. How's everything?'

Ben Gresham looked at her sharply. 'Everything or everyone or *someone*?' he asked pointedly.

Lynne found herself flushing. 'It was just a general question,' she retorted stiffly, 'but since you put it like that, how are Ron Jenkins and—Dr Layton?'

Ben Gresham smiled a trifle wryly. 'Ron Jenkins is making excellent progress and is the life and soul of the ward and keeps asking when his little red-headed nurse is coming to visit him!' He chuckled. 'I must say you must have made quite an impression on him. I must remember to ask him for the secret of his success. Oh, and you asked about old Timothy—I thought you would have enquired about him first. He's doing as well as can be expected—still has fits of headache and depression. Perhaps a visit from you would cheer him up in the circumstances.'

'What circumstances do you mean, Ben Gresham?' Lynne had demanded heatedly before she realised the trap set for her.

'Oh, just something a junior bird told me,' Ben said airily. 'Remember you did say that I would know about situations like that. I've been pondering over that remark ever since. Just exactly what did you mean?'

'Simply that the junior nurse started to say something about no visitors and Dr Layton told her his fiancée was just leaving,' Lynne told him wearily. 'Nothing more than the usual visitor's excuse for five more minutes.'

'And you expect me to believe that?' Ben's voice lifted in apparent astonishment.

Lynne fought to restrain her anger and the welcome sound of the telephone in the office rescued her.

'Dr Gresham has just left,' she told Switchboard. 'No, there isn't a casualty. Dr Gresham thought he had left some notes here.'

'Thank you, Staff Nurse. I quite understand. By the way, welcome back to St David's.'

The receiver clicked in her ear and Lynne replaced the phone. That last little remark had taken the sting out of her anger and she could have only imagined that there was any significance in what the man had said first. She was getting far too sensitive, taking idle remarks at far above their real value. Perhaps that junior had been right—she really *was* suffering from delayed shock without knowing it. There didn't have to be nightmares and twitchings. For a long moment Lynne longed to throw up her chosen career and to phone Aunt Jenny and tell her she would love to come on that dream tour . . .

When the junior float turned up at ten o'clock to let Lynne go to first supper, she couldn't help listening with sharpened attention to the younger girl's voice. Was she called Janie or was she the speaker?

'It's nice to see you back, Staff Nurse. It must have been terrible for you.'

Unexpectedly Lynne found the attention more embarrassing than being ignored. 'I'd rather not talk about it, Nurse!' she said crushingly. 'Dr Gresham is on for Casualty if a case comes in, and you know where I'll be.' She had walked through the door before the astonished hurt on the young face had registered. It was too late to apologise now. She would have to make it up to the girl when she came back from supper. This certainly wasn't a good start to her first night on. She had snapped Ben Gresham's head off for simply being himself and she had been beastly to a junior, and she knew just how much that could hurt.

Lynne had finished her first cup of tea when she was summoned back. The casualty was an apologetic elderly woman.

'So sorry to be bothering you at this hour, Nurse. Never happened to me before—filled that bottle a hundred times without a splash, and this time I has to pour it over my hand! I wouldn't have bothered you, but the lady in the next flat happened to hear me and she brought me.'

Lynne sent the junior to make the two old ladies cups of tea and laid out the burns tray while she waited for Ben.

He arrived at the same time as the tea. 'Two more cups, there's a dear,' he ordered cheerfully, 'and we'll have a nice little tea-party—don't forget yourself. What have we here, Staff Nurse? Dear, dear, that's a nasty one.' His voice was as gentle as his hands and he kept up his chatter while he cleaned the burn and did the dressing. Both the old ladies were chuckling at his jokes and colour had come back into their lined faces.

Lynne found herself sipping tea with her junior and smiling at Ben Gresham's foolery. She had to admit that there was no harm in him at this moment and probably a lot of good. Perhaps daytime pressures did make too many of them work to rules and humaneness got left outside the doors. Ben Gresham insisted upon driving the old ladies home even though they said it was only a step.

'Someone might make a pass at you both!'

They were highly flattered. 'Not unless you do, Doctor.'

Lynne started to clear away the dressing tray. 'Thanks for making the tea, Nurse.' She smiled as she said it, wishing she could remember the girl's name.

'Dad's been asking if you could call round to see him, Staff Nurse,' the junior asked shyly.

Lynne stared at her. 'You're Nurse Jenkins, then. I didn't know. He didn't say any of you were old enough—' her voice trailed off.

The young face was very flushed. 'Mum and I don't know how to thank you, Staff Nurse. I tried to say it earlier—'

Bitterly ashamed, Lynne smiled at her reassuringly. 'You can thank me best by going off to your supper, Nurse Jenkins. Tell your father I'll try to see him to-morrow.' Her tone was crisp, but the younger girl only beamed happily before hurrying away.

Lynne slowly restored the dressing room to its customary neatness and took the empty cups through to the kitchen. She had never in her life before done something in the line of duty that had involved her with so many separate lives. It looked like being a long time before the various strands were unravelled.

Lynne had two more simple casualties before midnight—a hand cut on a broken bottle and an eye badly bruised by a hasty fist. There was no need to call back Nurse Jenkins and Ben was tied up in theatre, so Lynne dealt efficiently with them on her own, the policemen who had brought the two youths in being only too happy to help with the bandaging. This time Lynne went and made the cups of tea without any hints being thrown. She was learning fast that night duty in Casualty involved social service as well as medical attention.

It was three o'clock when the phone went, rousing Lynne from her weary struggle against sleep. 'Casualty, Staff Nurse Howard speaking.' She hoped she sounded more awake than she felt.

'Night Sister here. Nurse Jenkins is on her way down

to you. I want you to come over to the Neuro Block immediately.'

Lynne found herself stammering. 'What—for, Sister? Where am I to come to?'

'I think you know very well, Staff Nurse—the side ward where Dr Layton is. Don't wait for the junior float.'

This time Lynne went to the Neuro Block by the official route. To her relief there was no sign of the junior nurse who had been on duty the other night.

Night Sister was waiting outside the side ward and her face was worried under its grimness. 'Dr Layton seems to be reliving his experiences in the tunnel. He's had a sedative, but it doesn't appear to be having any effect. So go in and sit with him until he quietens down. It doesn't matter *what* you say or do, provided it has the right result!'

Lynne was too startled to take in the real significance of her senior's words or even to wonder why she should make such a remark. She opened the door. The room was in semi-darkness, but this only served to make the torment of the man thrashing about in the bed more terrifying. He was speaking in a rapid undertone.

'Why haven't you got your boots on, you silly little fool? If you hadn't been late on duty we'd have got the men out by now. Look out! The roof's coming down!'

Lynne caught at the clutching hands and tried to soothe the distraught man. 'It's all right, Dr Layton. It's all right. There's no one in the tunnel now. Everyone's safe. Everyone's safe—quite safe.' Over and over again she repeated the words, trying to get through to the tortured brain.

Timothy Layton eased himself back on the pillow, but his hands held Lynne's so tightly that she almost cried out. 'Why did you go away and leave me? You should have stayed, Sarah. You know how much your red hair fascinates me, how much I love you—'

A sudden gasp behind her brought Lynne out of her bewildered daze.

'I thought you told me there was *no* situation, Lynne. It would seem that you lied to your Uncle Ben.'

And then there was the sound of the door being closed softly and Lynne was left staring at the man in the bed— the man whose eyes were completely blank as he murmured over and over again:

'Sarah, don't leave me again—I love you so much.'

# CHAPTER FOUR

Lynne was cold and her eyelids was smarting with the effort to stay awake. Timothy Layton was asleep now, but still restless, and his grip on Lynne's hands had only slackened slightly. She couldn't see her watch and she was sure she had been there for simply hours and hours.

She was roused by a slight touch on her shoulder. Night Sister was standing beside her. The older woman leaned down and expertly released Lynne's fingers. The sleeping man moved, but didn't waken.

'Come along, Staff Nurse. He should sleep for several hours.'

Lynne obeyed. She ached in every bone as she tried to subdue her shivering. Night Sister halted her in the corridor.

'Better make yourself some tea when you get back to Casualty, Staff Nurse.' She looked at Lynne curiously. 'I don't understand what you see in the man, myself. He's much older than you are, too.'

Lynne tried to murmur a reply, but her lips seemed too stiff to form any words. In any case she didn't think the older woman would believe her. Timothy Layton in his delirium or out of it had done his job too well.

To her relief Nurse Jenkins went off again to help on the wards without any questions or enquiring glances. Perhaps Lynne would be allowed to get through the night without anything else happening, but Ben Gresham and fate decided otherwise.

The police brought in the victim of a hit-and-run and of course the accident had to happen just outside St

David's. Not even an ambulance had to be called, only the night porter and a stretcher.

Ben Gresham came down to Casualty. He was rubbing his eyes, and blue stripes showing above his white coat suggested that he had made some attempt to go to bed.

'What now, Staff Nurse? I thought we'd made an agreement.' Then he seemed to wake up properly, gave Lynne a rather hurt look, and went efficiently about his task of assessing the man's injuries. They had to wait for the X-ray technician to turn up, then another interval while the girl developed the plates.

Ben surveyed the dripping films. 'Could be a hairline fracture. We'd better take him in for observation.'

It was six-thirty by the time the man had been dispatched up to an emergency bed hastily erected in one of the wards. The police had got their details and departed. Lynne had tidied up once again, while Ben was sitting by the dressing trolley writing up the notes.

Lynne finished what she was doing and suddenly became aware that Ben was simply sitting there watching her.

'Well, Lynne, don't you think you owe me an explanation? I never expected you of all people to tell me a lie.'

Weary as she was, Lynne felt warm anger flood through her. 'I don't suppose it ever occurred to you that there could be another redhead in Timothy Layton's life!' she said hotly.

'Quite frankly it hasn't, and I wouldn't believe it.'

Lynne fought for calmness. 'I'm not in the habit of lying, Dr Gresham! Her name is Sarah and some time in the past she went away and left him—so there!' Inexplicably she felt a pang of betrayal. This time she had made an impression.

'So that's why they asked me what your first name

was, or rather whether you had another Christian name. How did you find out about this other girl?'

Lynne steadied her voice. 'In his delirium he kept begging this Sarah person to come back, that's all.' The fact that Timothy Layton loved this unknown girl was his secret, not hers. If the rest of the staff on Neuro had heard him raving—well, it was their business.

'How about a cup of tea, Lynne, just to show you don't hold it against me for doubting your veracity?'

Lynne smiled tiredly. 'Big words for this hour of the morning. Do you mind coming through for it? I don't think I'd have the strength to walk this way again.'

Ben was all concern. 'I bet it's all of two years since you've done night duty. I guess you're not weaned to this no sleep lark. I know I used to feel about ninety come the dawn. How long are you going to be on nights, anyway?'

Lynne stifled a yawn. 'Only a few nights, I think.' She remembered the scene in the side ward. Perhaps Matron would leave her even longer when she heard what had happened. It would depend upon Night Sister's version—and so many things could be misinterpreted and, no doubt, would be.

'Thanks for the tea, little one. Your Uncle Ben will now have the strength to stagger back to sweet bed for what's left of the dawn.'

As if to mock his words a finger of sunlight began to light up the tall windows of the main waiting hall.

'I think you're a little late for that, Ben,' Lynne said gravely. A load seemed to slip from her shoulders. That ghastly first night was almost over.

Ben Gresham groaned. 'So it would seem. Sweet dreams, Lynne, and if you wake, think of me staggering round coping with an endless stream of casualties. See you the night after next. Tonight I'll toss a coin to see whether I shall sleep the sleep of blissful not being on call or hit the high spots with our Bibs.'

But Lynne was too weary even to rise to that final jibe. 'Thanks, Ben—for everything.'

She didn't wait for his reply but walked towards the office to complete her record of the night's casualties. There was one item that she wouldn't put down—the summons to the Neuro Block. Her thought wasn't strong enough to switch on memory. Too much had happened, and tonight would be just another night to be endured.

Lynne broke St David's unwritten rule and didn't go over to the dining room for breakfast. All she wanted was a slow warm bath and a long, long sleep. She wouldn't admit even to herself that she might be avoiding unwelcome comment on what had gone on in the side ward on the Neuro Block.

As she opened her bedroom door the spicy scent of autumn flowers came out to meet her. Every available vase seemed to hold chrysanthemums—great golden once, lacy pink ones with long shaggy petals, delicate white globes of fluff, and the tiny miniature ones. Slowly, very slowly, Lynne took in their beauty and then began to look for a card for some hint as to the donor. There were three cards, they all bore the same surname—Jenkins—and their message was one of warm gratitude, affection even, and the smarting pain of the past few days vanished. Lynne was humming a little tune to herself as she went for her bath. Life wasn't too bad after all. If she woke up early enough she could slip over to the men's ward to see Ron Jenkins.

Friday night began all wrong for Lynne. She got on duty to discover that the day staff's casualties were flooding over into her spell of duty. The plaster room doors were open to reveal bowls and buckets full of the remains of plaster bandages, and liquid plaster had flowed everywhere. A flustered junior was trying to introduce a little order into the mess. Groups of relatives were sitting in tired groups on the benches and a couple of ambulance men stood just outside the casualty entrance snatching a quick smoke. A burst of laughter from the direction of the office suggested that Junior Staff Nurse Barbara Stanwell was holding court with at least two house surgeons.

Lynne baulked at the correct procedure which should have forced her to break up that merry group. Instead she moved quietly among the waiting people, filling herself in on the details of the accidents. She sent the junior to the kitchen to make everyone a strong cup of tea. Then with the expertness of long practice she reduced the plaster room to its proper orderliness. By the time the office door opened to release two somewhat hilarious and flushed house surgeons Lynne was just putting her mop and bucket back in the porter's cupboard and the junior was collecting the last of the cups. The two men gave Lynne a cheery wave of the hand but didn't stop to speak.

Lynne walked towards the office as Barbara Stanwell emerged, adjusting her cap as she came. She looked startled and somewhat flustered as she saw Lynne. She had the grace to flush as she took in the fact that no junior, however efficient, could have restored the department to its present neatness.

'You should have told me you were here, Staff Nurse!' She made a show of blustering her way out of the situation.

Lynne refused to rise to the attack. 'You must have had a hectic time. Anything special to report?'

The younger girl shrugged her shoulders. 'Two patients still in X-Ray. They've been taking ages down there. I can't think why these people are still waiting.'

One of the women sitting within earshot spoke up. 'I

can tell you why, Nurse—'cos you couldn't be bothered
to come and let us know whether we had to wait or not.
Too busy a-laughing and carrying on with them young
doctors, you were. You ought to be ashamed of yourself!'

Lynne took pity on the discomfited girl. 'I'll deal with
it. You don't want to be too late for your date with—'
She stopped abruptly. Ben could have been only teasing.

Barbara Stanwell gave her a furious glance and
snatched up her cloak and hurried out of the department.

The woman who had spoken before chuckled. 'You
were too soft with her, Staff Nurse. It's her kind what
give Casualty a bad name.'

The return of the two patients from X-Ray saved
Lynne the embarrassment of replying. The ambulance
drivers came forward and under their shepherding guid-
ance the hall was miraculously cleared. Lynne gave a
sigh of relief and went into the office to read the day
report. There was a timid tap on the door and the day
junior came in cautiously.

'I've brought you some tea, Staff Nurse, and thanks
for doing the plaster room for me.'

Lynne gave her a surprised smile. 'Thank *you* for the
tea, Nurse Ryan. I expect you're more than ready to go
off duty.'

'I am! We haven't stopped since tea-time.' She turned
to go and then glanced back shyly. 'I wish you were back
on days, Staff Nurse!' She scuttled away like a frightened
mouse.

Lynne poured herself out a cup of tea and echoed the
junior's wish. She hoped and prayed that she would be
back on days in time for the weekend. It was Sister
Casualty's turn to be off and normally Lynne stood in for
her. If only she could be sure that the wretched Bibs

wouldn't be allowed to stand in! A thought struck her and she went over to look at the off-duty rota, but Sister Casualty must have been too busy to alter it. The list was just as it had been before this week had ever started. The Admin. Office must have been given a daily list, and Lynne was no wiser. She would have to wait for Sister Casualty to tell her in the morning. Somehow she didn't see herself putting the fateful question.

To Lynne's surprise and relief the night was quiet; apart from two emergency appendix cases who were whisked through her department straight to theatre. It must have been busy on the wards as well, because Lynne had no visitors, not even a thirsty house surgeon or a medical student in search of a cup of tea or a quick snack. Nurse Jenkins must have had a night off, because it was another junior who came down to relieve Lynne for supper and she was half an hour late.

'Sorry, Staff Nurse, but we've had two theatre cases!' she apologised breathlessly. 'Anything you want me to do while you're at supper?'

'Sit yourself down, Nurse, and if you feel too guilty at having a rest, you can cut out some of those anaesthetic lint eye-shields. I won't count how many you do.' Lynne hurried away before she revealed just how lonely she had been in the echoing emptiness of Casualty.

By the time three o'clock came Lynne was eyeing the phone, wondering if it would ring like last night. There hadn't been a chance to ask anyone whether Dr Timothy Layton was better or not. Ben Gresham would have been the only person she would have risked questioning. At least he had appeared to accept that there might be another red-headed girl in the Senior Casualty Officer's life.

When the time came to hand the department back to

Sister Casualty there were still no more than two names in the report.

To Lynne's relief Sister Casualty seemed more at ease. 'So you had a quiet night, Staff Nurse. Just as well, perhaps, since Matron would like to see you at nine o'clock. You won't have an excuse to miss your breakfast this morning.'

Lynne felt as guilty as any junior, but the faint twinkle in the older woman's eyes suggested that she understood. Lynne wished she could be sure that Matron was going to let her come back on day duty. This week's events had severely shaken the old relationship between Sister Casualty and her senior staff nurse, and Lynne wondered if she would ever feel as secure again. Perhaps her godmother had been right—there were other things in life than jobs and careers.

Matron's face was very thoughtful as she surveyed Lynne standing stiffly to attention in front of her desk.

'I think it might be better in the present circumstances that you go back on day duty in Casualty, Staff Nurse. At least you will be too busy to get involved in unusual happenings.' There had been the suggestion of a pause between those last two words. Lynne wondered miserably what sort of report Night Sister had handed in. 'You had better sit down, Staff Nurse. There are one or two things we need to discuss. I have heard something that has rather disturbed me concerning you and a member of the medical staff. No doubt Night Sister acted as she thought fit in very difficult circumstances. However, her action has brought a degree of publicity to a situation I think all of us would have preferred to keep private. I must confess I was surprised. I am usually aware of emotional or romantic happenings that go on in this hospital far sooner than most people imagine.'

Lynne sat very still. She must find the right words this

time. 'Matron, I assure you that at no time has there been any kind of a relationship other than a professional one.' The astonishment on Matron's face almost unnerved her, but Lynne managed to continue. 'I can only say that when Night Sister left me with Dr Layton he wasn't calling for me but for someone called Sarah. I don't know anything else except that she has red hair and is—very dear to him.' Her cheeks were flushed as she looked appealingly at Matron. 'That's all there is to it.'

The older woman was silent for what seemed a very long time. 'I must accept what you say, Staff Nurse. I can't see your reason for lying when such a story can be checked when Dr Layton is better, should such checking be necessary. Of course Dr Layton hasn't been with us very long and naturally his private life is his own affair.' She sighed. 'I suppose it's understandable how the error arose, but unfortunate nonetheless. I must admit that quite frankly I am thankful that we won't have to change our plans for Casualty, as we would have if there had been romance in the air.' Matron smiled a little and Lynne felt like doing a dance from sheer relief. 'Oh, I understand that Staff Nurse Stanwell was exceedingly late getting off duty last night.' She looked enquiringly at Lynne.

'There was a hold-up in X-Ray, Matron, but I helped with the clearing up as soon as I got on duty,' Lynne said diplomatically. There was absolutely nothing to be gained by mentioning that her help had not been returned. Dear Bibs would-hang herself in due course without any assistance from anyone.

'I'm sure you did. Now, if you can get some sleep this morning and go on at two p.m., Sister Casualty will be able to go off on her weekend as planned. Thank you very much for being so frank with me, Staff Nurse. The situation couldn't have been either easy or pleasant for you, and the fact that Dr Layton is a good deal better today suggests that you managed to deal very efficiently with the matter.'

Lynne felt she was floating all the way to the Nurses' Home. She longed to share the good news with someone, but Ben Gresham would be busy. Aunt Jenny would probably tease her, and anyway what had happened came under the heading of confidential patient-nurse relationships. Perhaps she shouldn't even have told Ben, but it had been essential that someone believed her.

Lynne was sure that she would be too excited to sleep, but the loud shrilling of her alarm clock proved her wrong. Dazedly she lifted her head and stared round her room. The vases of flowers from the Jenkins family looked forlornly back at her and reminded her that she had intended to replenish their water when she got off duty.

Lynne had slept too heavily to feel like lunch. Switching back to day duty was almost as painful as going on nights. Perhaps she would go over to Aunt Jenny's. If it happened to be one of Mrs Jenkins' days she could thank her for the flowers. She still hadn't managed to call at the ward to see Ron Jenkins. No doubt someone would have told her if he wasn't going on all right.

It was Mrs Jenkins who opened the door to Lynne. 'Oh, it's you, Nurse. Mrs Leslie should be back soon. I've just lighted the fire. I'm sure Mrs Leslie wouldn't mind if I made you a cuppa.'

'I'd love one,' Lynne said simply. 'And thank you all for those lovely flowers. You shouldn't have done it.'

'I left it to our Jessie to get them. If you hadn't done what you did, Nurse, we'd have been buying them for my Ron. Seems only right we should do a little something to say thanks. I'll be making that cuppa, Nurse.'

Lynne smiled a little as she went through to the lounge. Nurses might grumble about unappreciative patients, but it seemed that gratitude could be an embarrassment all round. She had finished browsing through her godmother's magazines by the time Aunt Jenny returned.

'I thought you might be dropping in, Lynne. I was wondering how you were getting on. Mrs Jenkins is making a tray of tea before she goes. I see she gave you one to go on with.' Jenny Leslie unloaded her parcels and sat down opposite Lynne with a sigh. 'Shopping gets more of a bore every time! I wish they'd invent push-button shopping!'

Lynne laughed. 'And you'd miss all the fun of trying things on. Did you buy anything exciting?'

'Only necessities—underwear and so on. I'm waiting to decide when and where to go for my winter holiday. Wish you'd give up your job and come with me.'

'If I'd had to stay on nights I might have, but Matron's put me back on days. I have to be on at two o'clock,' Lynne explained.

'You mean you can't stay for tea? What about lunch, or did you go over to the dining room?'

Lynne shook her head. 'I didn't feel like any, thanks all the same.'

'If you're quite sure—there's bound to be something in the fridge. Oh, any news of your Dr Layton?'

Lynne suddenly remembered that her godmother knew nothing of Thursday night's episode on the Neuro Block. Inexplicably she decided not to share it with the older woman. 'Matron said he was getting better,' she said evasively. 'Why?'

'Just curious. I have an idea that he was at university at the same time as John.' Once again she volunteered no further information. 'I don't want to hurry you, dear, but it's a quarter to two.'

Lynne jumped to her feet. 'Thanks for the cuppa. Be seeing you.'

'Drop round when you have a moment.'

Sister Casualty was waiting for Lynne and there was no sign of Junior Staff Nurse Barbara Stanwell. As if she had read Lynne's thought, 'I've sent Junior Staff Nurse to lunch. Shut the door. We might just get five minutes' peace. I must admit I'm very thankful you're back on day duty.' Sister chuckled a trifle wearily. 'I don't think I was aware of how much you saved me from until this week.' She gave Lynne a sharp glance. 'How often have you covered up for our young friend's deficiencies?' She saw Lynne's flush. 'All right, I shouldn't have asked. I suppose one of these days she'll settle down, or else one of her young men will do it for her. In my day—' Then she laughed at herself. 'I suppose I was just as bad, but I think I wasn't quite so noisy about it. I trust you won't have too busy a weekend. With Dr Layton still on the sick list I don't suppose they'll overburden us with casualties. You might go through the emergency drums—there hasn't been time to check them.'

With a distinct sense of shock Lynne realised that the episode of the tunnel wasn't yet a week ago. Sister Casualty didn't linger, and Lynne was glad. It was enough to be back on their old friendly footing without going into the reasons that had upset their working relationship.

She went in search of the two juniors clearing up after the morning session. They greeted her warmly.

'It's so nice to have you back, Staff Nurse. Bibs said you mightn't be coming, and it frightened us because she was so pleased about it.'

Lynne attempted to hide her pleasure and her surprise. 'Well, I'm back, so you'd better go to lunch.'

'But we've had ours, Staff Nurse. We were off duty this morning.'

No wonder Sister Casualty had looked weary. She must have managed the cases with only Bibs to assist her. So that was how she had discovered the girl's shortcomings.

'So Junior Staff has a half day then and—'

'—she isn't on until two p.m. tomorrow,' the two juniors interrupted with scant respect.

Lynne pretended to scold them, but she was too pleased to be back on day duty to put much severity into it. She left the juniors to get on with their own work and went to tackle the emergency drums. She was finishing repacking the last of them when Ben found her.

'I suppose this means you won't be keeping me company this evening, Lynne. I was counting on you.' He swung himself up on to the trolley.

'Have you had to change your weekend off, Ben?'

'Sort of—at least I have to be on for second call. Can't let a Junior House Officer take anything big—at least not by the rule book. With old Timothy likely to be away for a bit I can't see my off-duty improving. Pity I'm not on overtime rates!'

'With the new increases you'll be all right,' Lynne teased him.

'I suppose you want caviare and all the trimmings the next time I take you out,' Ben retorted.

'Next time? There hasn't been a first time so far!' Lynne retorted.

Ben took a notebook out of his pocket and flipped over the pages. 'So I haven't—I wonder why. Did you turn me down or something?'

Lynne laughed. 'Nothing like being given the chance! I was only teasing. Aren't you pleased about the new salary scales, then?'

Ben shrugged his shoulders. 'It only puts up my income tax, superannuation, and board, etc. Now I should find me a pretty working bird and see whether that changes the figures. It would have to be one with her own flat, because I'd still be charged for board here. You can't win, Lynne. I think I'll head for the Colonies.'

'Haven't you heard? There aren't any colonies left!'

'Well, whatever they call them nowadays. But seriously, I'd much rather stay in this country given half a chance. It makes me sick the way the powers-that-be mess us about. We would be able to man our own hospitals without bringing in outsiders, if they gave us the pay and the opportunities!'

'You mean if the NHS looked after British nationals only?' Lynne was a trifle surprised by Ben's heat. He seldom seemed to take things seriously.

'Something like that. Trouble is that Britain has been Mother Bountiful ever since the British Empire began, and now when she can't afford it she doesn't want to admit it or be thought mean. Silly, isn't it? We give millions for things that won't last and not even pennies for the things that build the future, like medical research or the nation's health. Someone's got the priorities all wrong.' He swung down off the trolley. 'End of lecture by Dr Ben Gresham. Well, I suppose I'd better do a ward round for the lucky blighters who *have* got the weekend off. Shout if you need me.' He walked towards the door. 'Oh, by the way, Timothy has been let out to convalesce.'

Lynne saw that he was watching her closely. 'I thought they kept head injuries under observation for longer,' she said non-committally. 'Has he gone away, then?'

'I thought you would be the first to know. He's staying with your friend, Mrs Leslie.'

# CHAPTER FIVE

LYNNE was too startled by Ben Gresham's news to attempt to hide her surprise. 'You must have it all wrong, Ben. I was over there only this afternoon.'

'Visiting old Timothy? You do keep astonishing me!'

Lynne glared at him. 'You know perfectly well I mean Aunt Jenny's! She would have mentioned it—' Lynne stopped abruptly, remembering her godmother's unfinished remark about John Leslie having been at university with Timothy Layton.

'What's up?' Ben regarded Lynne's flushed face with quizzical interest. 'I suppose you've just realised that old Timothy and your very attractive godmother are much of an age. I admit I don't know her very well, but I imagine quite a few men would regard her as quite a catch.'

Lynne was no longer listening. Not five minutes ago Ben had been talking about looking for a working girl with her own flat. Maybe he would regard an attractive widow with a flat plus private means as even better. The very thought gave her an odd little ache that had no physical source. For the moment she had completely forgotten that Timothy Layton was the actual person involved.

Ben became aware of Lynne's inattention and swung to his feet. 'Well, this isn't getting my ward rounds done.' He started towards the door, then came back and patted Lynne on the shoulder. 'Take a tip from your Uncle Ben and stop worrying about things that may never happen.'

He didn't linger to watch the fresh tide of colour sweep over Lynne's face nor to interpret her murmured protest.

Lynne's thoughts for the rest of her shift of duty were very mixed ones—a jumble of conjecture as to why Aunt Jenny should involve herself with the welfare of Timothy Layton or how the shy Senior Casualty Officer had overcome his diffidence sufficiently to accept such an invitation. Perhaps the blow on his head had resulted in a personality change. Unexpectedly Lynne caught herself remembering that brief but strange episode in the side ward of the Neuro Block. Should she warn her godmother?—but that was ridiculous. As far as she could tell Timothy Layton's feelings for the hardhearted, red-headed Sarah had been buried deep for a very long time. Breaking her nurse's code and putting Aunt Jenny in the picture presupposed that the older woman was doing more than offering hospitality to a colleague of her late husband.

Lynne was thankful when a string of minor casualties occupied her until the end of her duty period. Dressing gravel grazes and comforting crying children was a good antidote for an overdose of introspection.

Lynne found a phone message from Mrs Leslie when she got off duty. For a moment she contemplated ignoring it, but the old affection for her godmother was too strong and she joined the queue for the phone. The girls waiting were mostly juniors and shy enough to content themselves with smiles rather than conversation. One of them insisted on giving up her place to Lynne.

She brushed aside Lynne's protests. 'It's all right, Staff Nurse. You'll probably be quicker than me,' and then went scarlet.

Lynne chuckled at the girl's discomposure. 'So you don't think I'll be indulging in love talk! Never mind, I'm not, this time.' Her own colour was a trifle deeper when she went into the kiosk. So at twenty-three the juniors were busy crossing her off the list of rivals for the attentions of the medical staff and all . . .

Jenny Leslie's voice sounded quite unchanged when she answered. 'Hello, dear. I wasn't sure what time you would be off. I was wondering if you'd like to come over tomorrow evening. I'm having a few people in for supper and I thought it might be fun—unless you're going home.'

Lynne made an attempt to gather her wits. It was no business of hers to advise her godmother that people with head injuries should be kept very quiet. 'Yes, I'd love to come, Aunt Jenny.' At least she would be able to satisfy her curiosity. It was *only* curiosity, she told herself firmly. 'What time do you want me to come? I'm off at five, so I could give you a hand.'

The older woman laughed. 'I'm asking you as a guest, not as cheap labour! I've done most of the cooking today, so there will only be the buffet to arrange tomorrow. Any time after eight will do.'

Lynne put down the phone. On reflection the invitation, as well as the conversation, was remarkably similar to the many others she had had with her godmother ever since she had been at St David's. There was nothing to suggest that anything out of the ordinary had happened—nothing at all.

It was eight o'clock when Lynne stood in front of her mirror tucking in the last red curl. Even to her own critical gaze the dark blue dress with its touches of white braid on the hem and neckline and the pert matching jacket made her look quite different from that senior staff nurse, Lynne Howard. Perhaps a psychiatrist would read something into her choice of colours, but her own retort would be that with red hair you left the way-out clothes for the blondes and the brunettes. Idly she wondered who would be at the supper party. Often Aunt Jenny invited friends from her husband's department at the university, but she had a habit of mixing them with writers or singers or even a guitar player just to give a different flavour to the occasion. Good food and good talk well mixed up with a touch of spice was the recipe for the older woman's very successful parties.

It was Mrs Jenkins who opened the door to Lynne. 'My, but you do look pretty, Nurse! Mrs Leslie said I was to show the ladies to her bedroom, but I expect you knows the way. There's three or four here already, so you're to go through once you've left your coat.'

Lynne hesitated outside the door to the lounge. Mrs Jenkins' presence suggested that it might be a larger party than usual, or else there could be strangers demanding extra attention from their hostess.

As Lynne slipped into the room she glanced cautiously around looking for someone she knew. To her astonishment the first person she saw was Ben. He came bounding happily to meet her.

'Thank goodness you've come, Lynne. There are too many goldfish in this bowl for my liking, and we don't seem to use the same language.'

'I thought you and Timothy would know what to talk about,' Lynne said rather caustically. She wasn't being quite fair to Ben. It was Aunt Jenny who kept springing the surprises.

'Old Timothy? Haven't laid an eye on him. Perhaps your godmother is keeping him as the *pièce de résistance*—pardon my French.'

'What for? Your accent's almost as good as those I heard in Paris,' Lynne retorted.

'Stop showing off. How about a drink? A sherry, or a

fancy cocktail with a nice cherry on a stick?'

'Sherry, please. Where's Aunt Jenny?'

'Over in the corner with a minor celebrity. She'll see you later. I have my instructions to look after you.'

Lynne accepted the glass of sherry. 'Thanks a lot—thanks for everything, but I can look after myself if you want to browse.'

Ben glanced at her reproachfully. 'I would far rather look after thee, my pretty. Let me whisper in your little ear that thou art the fairest by far.'

Lynne flushed at this nonsense, but she was quite pleased. Breaking the ice at a party was far pleasanter done in twos.

Ben found them a cosy little corner with a small table for their drinks, collecting a few dishes of titbits on the way.

'Help yourself, Lynne. Anything else you fancy?'

'Don't eat too much, Ben. Aunt Jenny's buffets are famous for their eatability! So save some space.'

Ben scooped up a handful of nuts and munched them thoughtfully. 'It's been a busy day, little one, and your Uncle Ben never did get to the dining room. Too late for breakfast—a blocked intravenous drip instead of lunch, and an emergency appendix chose dinner-time for attention. Did you work today? I tried to head in that direction a couple of times, but always got waylaid.'

Lynne held up her glass. 'Of course I did—the usual Sunday cleaning. Cheers. This is supposed to be a party, not a case history of the day's work.'

'Sorry, Lynne. Uncle Ben doesn't get to many parties, so he's no good at small talk. You'll have to talk for both of us—spill out the usual chit-chat.'

Mrs Leslie came bustling over. 'So glad you're here, Lynne. I hope Ben is looking after you properly. Lucas is dealing with the wine, so as soon as Mrs Jenkins brings in the casseroles we'll be ready to eat. Juan is going to play his guitar, and that should liven things up a little.'

Lynne watched her godmother walk through the various groups, no doubt making a similar announcement, and thought she had never seen her look more attractive.

'It must be a lonely life for her,' Ben commented.

Lynne's hand trembled a little and she put down her glass. 'She has her voluntary work, but I suppose it can't be all parties for her. I expect I've always envied her in a way, so I didn't think about it like that,' she said carefully.

'Don't take it so seriously. I was only keeping up my end of the conversation!' Ben protested. 'Why is it that we do far better with a patient between us?'

Lynne had to smile. 'Never mind, Ben. Look, that must be Juan what's-his-name. If he's anything like the others of Aunt Jenny's collection he should be good.'

The first low strumming notes of the guitar broke up the patterns of conversation as people turned to look at the dark young man standing by the buffet in the bow window. Behind him the dark red velvet curtains drawn against the chill of the autumn darkness showed off the richness of the embroidery on his waistcoat. Then the playing began in earnest and the throbbing notes seemed to fill the room with a fire as bright as the one glowing on the hearth. After the passionate introduction Juan's playing slowed to a quiet trickle of background music and Mrs Leslie urged her guests to help themselves.

'Don't stand on ceremony, and there's plenty more to come. Tell Lucas whether you want white or red wine, or you can stick to your sherry or cocktails.'

Lynne and Ben held back until the worst of the crush round the buffet had subsided.

'Stay here, Lynne, and trust your Uncle Ben to bring

something you fancy, eh? Just say if there's anything you don't like.'

Lynne stood up and gazed over at the array still so tempting in spite of the hungry inroads already made. Peeping out of surrounds of snowy napkins were appetising piles of chicken vol-au-vents, baked potatoes, and crusty rolls. Savoury steam rose from dishes of cheese fondue sitting over flickering nightlights. There were various casseroles perched on a warming table each looking more exciting than the last. Platters of hors-d'œuvres were arranged together with bowls of green salad and a plate of cold meats for those who preferred plainer living.

Lynne sighed in happy anticipation. 'I'll leave the choice to you, Ben. It all looks out of this world. I only wish St David's Catering Officer could see what can be done with food!'

While Ben was looking after the gastronomic side of their evening Lynne gazed round at the various little groups. Some of the faces were vaguely familiar, and the topics—love or politics or scientific discoveries or the latest books, plays, shows, or songs—were all ones she had heard before, but how remote they all seemed from life within the walls of St David's.

Ben returned with a laden tray and began to move the items over to the comparative smallness of their table. Know something, Lynne? I have a feeling we've moved over to another planet, or else St David's is out of this world, like one of those old monasteries or something. I've been listening to the chatter—no, it's more serious than chatter, to them at any rate. I can remember conversations like that when I was at university—dead serious, with a revolution just around the corner or the end of the world due any second now. I'd like to take a handful of these people and set them down inside St

David's for twenty-four hours. Only then will they have lived!'

Lynne laughed. 'I was thinking the same—either *we're* too ignorant of what goes on in the world to be turned loose or else *they're* full of nothing but theories and vague goodwill.'

'And here I thought you were nothing but a good-looking bird thinking only of the next shift of duty! Lynne, you surprise me! Start on that cheese fondue while I get us some wine. White—not too sweet?'

Lynne nodded. Juan was playing more loudly now, the volume of his melody just below the level of conversation, so that it teased at one's attention, adding to the unreality of this departure from her everyday routine. She looked up and caught the mocking admiring glance of Juan's dark eyes. Then Ben was back with their wine and she joined him in concentrating on the banquet in front of them.

Finally Ben sat back, licking his fingers appreciatively. He grinned at Lynne. 'Far too good to waste even a taste on a serviette! What would you like for afters? Fruit or an ice, or both?'

Before Lynne could answer the door opened and a rather flustered Mrs Jenkins appeared looking anxiously for her employer. She caught sight of Lynne and came over.

'It's a call for Dr Timothy Layton, Nurse. Can't say I remembers anyone by that name. A Miss Sarah Somebody wants a word with him most urgent. Have you seen Mrs Leslie? I'm not one for pushing through so many.'

Ben and Lynne exchanged astonished glances, but before either of them could say anything Jenny Leslie was hurrying towards them and took Mrs Jenkins with her. However, both of them distinctly heard Lynne's godmother say:

'I did explain about pushing the buzzer, Mrs Jenkins, and then you switch the call through to the other flat.'

It was Ben Gresham who spoke. 'Curiouser and curiouser. I wonder what's up. Is there *another* flat?'

'I only know that the house was divided up, but I thought an elderly retired couple had it—Darrell, I think their name is.'

'Never mind, little one. I don't suppose it's any of our business—not mine, at any rate.' He looked questioningly at Lynne, but before she could answer, Mrs Jenkins came back into the room.

'Dr Gresham, you're wanted in Casualty. There's been a coach crash—children, they said, and something about a major alert.'

Ben was on his feet. 'Come on, Lynne, that means you as well. You can put a gown on over your party togs.'

There had been a ripple of attention through the room at Mrs Jenkins' dramatic entry and for a moment Juan stopped playing. Then as they went out of the front door the music rose in a demanding crescendo that climbed above the voices.

'See what I mean?' Ben said bitterly as he helped Lynne into his sports car. 'They don't want to know! Come on, Betsy girl, show your best speed,' and the elderly car roared into action.

They left it parked away from the Casualty entrance, the stream of ambulances warning them that every inch of space would be needed.

Ben tugged at Lynne's arm. 'This way—you can have a gown from the doctors' changing room.'

Feeling very much like a gaudy canary among the house sparrows, Lynne obeyed, and they managed to work their way round the crush of people thronging Casualty.

Safe behind the anonymity of a gown and surgical cap,

with a mask dangling round her neck, Lynne emerged from the changing room without waiting for Ben. She made herself a pathway through the crowd heading for the main Casualty Theatre where she could see the tall figure of Night Sister dealing with the stream of ambulance men and their stretchers coming through the Casualty entrance.

'Thank goodness you're here, Staff Nurse! We've sent six of the worst cases to the Theatre Block. If you and Dr Gresham will deal with this lot—they're mostly minor injuries from flying glass. Use local anaesthetic and spray-on dressings and they can be reviewed for further treatment once the worst of the crush is over. The house surgeon is splinting the fractures in the plaster room and sending them on to X-Ray. All right?'

Lynne and Ben found themselves firmly pushed into Casualty Theatre where two white-faced juniors were vainly trying to soothe the frightened, bewildered children.

Ben surveyed the room with an experienced eye. 'We'll take the big girl first. What's your name, beautiful? Suppose you tell us what happened?'

In seconds the room was quiet, Ben expertly assessing the girl's injuries as she told them of the coach skidding on a muddy stretch and turning over.

'A couple of fine stitches and a spray-on dressing, Staff Nurse,' Ben said softly. 'They can admit her to the Plastic Surgery Ward and Mr Reynolds will see her on his ward round tomorrow. There's nothing more we can do for her here—not and deal with the other kiddies.'

Slowly they worked their way through the room, quiet now as belated shock and weariness numbed the children to the frightening strangeness of their surroundings. Lynne sent one of the juniors to make the children warm drinks. The other junior fetched extra blankets and pillows from Stores. As Ben and Lynne finished dealing with each casualty the younger girl snuggled the child down with blankets and pillows. Some were asleep before their cocoa arrived, but no one was bothered.

Ben straightened up after lifting the last child from the theatre table. 'If that cup of cocoa is going spare I'll have it. What about you, Staff Nurse?'

Lynne absently tucked a stray curl back under her cap. She shuddered a little. 'Not now, thanks. I'd better see if Night Sister has anything else for us.'

She slipped through the door and the noisiness of the main Casualty hall struck at her ears like a blow. There were groups of patient ambulance men, but most of the adults were obviously anxious parents demanding to know the whereabouts of their children. There were a few reporters and cameramen, and Lynne was suddenly thankful for her disguise—they would take her for a doctor and respect the urgency of the occasion. She was surprised to see Matron and the House Governor standing with a couple of police inspectors, but there was no sign of Night Sister. Perhaps she would be in the office. Lynne made her way round the various groups, not wanting to be involved with public relations just yet. At least there were no more children waiting for attention. No doubt they were distributed round the smaller dressing rooms, admitted to the wards, or sent to Theatre or to X-Ray.

Lynne tapped on the half-closed office door and went in. To her astonishment it was Casualty Sister who sat behind the desk while Night Sister was on the phone.

The older woman silently invited Lynne to take a chair, but there was the flicker of an approving smile across her tired face.

Night Sister put the receiver down. 'They've put six cots up in the women's day room and they'll put more if we need them. Oh, there you are, Staff Nurse. How many of your cases need admission?'

Lynne started to get to her feet, but was firmly gestured back to her seat. 'There's one girl with fairly severe facial lacerations that Dr Gresham thinks should be admitted to the Plastic Surgery Ward, and about five other children. I think the rest can go home, but—'

'But what, Staff Nurse?'

Lynne hesitated. 'They're fast asleep,' she admitted reluctantly.

Sister Casualty gave a faint chuckle. 'I think you can trust the ambulance men not to waken them, Staff Nurse, but we'll have to let the parents in to identify them.'

Lynne fished a slip of paper out of her pocket. 'I'm afraid we couldn't make out all the surnames, but we have first names and approximate ages.'

Sister Casualty stood up. 'Give me that list, Staff Nurse. This *is* something I can deal with. Night Sister will arrange for a bed for the facial injuries case. Perhaps you would get a trolley and take the girl to the ward. If she has parents take them with you.'

Already the groups of people seemed smaller and one or two of the dressing room doors stood open, although there was still a queue outside the plaster room. Lynne left Sister Casualty reading out her list of names and went in search of a trolley.

She found Ben standing beside the big girl, who was sobbing quietly. He looked up with relief as he saw Lynne.

'This for Shirley? Good. I've given her a sedative, but it hasn't helped as yet.' He helped Lynne shift the girl over on to the trolley.

'What about your parents, Shirley? They can come up to the ward with you.'

The girl's sobbing stopped for a moment. 'Haven't got no parents. I live with my boy's auntie.' She began to cry again.

'Hush, Shirley. If you give us your boy-friend's name or his aunt's—'

'I don't want them to see me like this, not ever!'

'It'll be all right, Shirley, once it's healed,' Ben said with as much authority as he could manage.

'You're only saying that to make me feel good. I had a look when you were doing the kiddies. Save the lies for them, they might believe them!' The girl's desperate sobs began to quieten as the sedative took effect.

'Let's get her out of here,' Ben muttered.

Lynne took her final glance round the chaos, but the two juniors were looking after the only two casualties still awake. The sounds outside in the main hall suggested that Sister Casualty was bringing the parents this way.

'All right, Dr Gresham. We can make out her admission slip on the ward.' She was annoyed to detect an unsteady note in her voice.

Sister Casualty held back the wave of parents like a traffic warden to let them through with the trolley. She whispered in Lynne's ear, 'No parents here, only a very irate young man. I've put him in my office and I won't let him up until I've sorted out this lot.' She gave Lynne a gentle push. 'Away you go, Staff Nurse. You'll need all your strength in the morning.'

With a sense of shock Lynne saw that the big clock showed it was four o'clock. Had they really been here as long as that? The sag of Ben's shoulders as he guided the trolley suggested that indeed it had been a very long time.

It was four-thirty by the time they came back to Casualty to collect Lynne's coat. To their astonishment

the main hall was empty and only the distant clatter of
mop and bucket suggested that even the chaos in the
dressing rooms, Casualty Theatre and plaster room was
no more.

Ben untied the strings of Lynne's gown and helped her
on with her coat. Then he sat down heavily and pulled
out a packet of cigarettes. He stared at it for a moment,
then slammed it angrily on the table. 'I don't know why
the hell I ever took up this medical lark, and that's a fact!
Those people at your godmother's party knew what they
were doing. I'm the fool, not they. Oh, Lynne, that
child's face! I can't get it out of my mind—' He brushed
the back of his hand across his eyes rather sheepishly.
'Don't tell them that your Uncle Ben has gone soft, will
you, Lynne?' Then with a change of tone: 'Want me to
run you home?'

Lynne picked up her handbag. 'I'd have to get the
night porter to let me in, thanks all the same, Ben.'
Rather shyly she rested her hand on his shoulder. 'Don't
let it get you, Ben. Mr Reynolds is pretty good on faces.'

He reached up and put his own hand over hers. 'Bless
you, Lynne. It was only what the kid's going through
now.'

'I know, but at least she'll wake up to find her boy-
friend sitting beside her. I suspect he's interested in
more than just a pretty face.'

'Off you go, Lynne, or it will be breakfast time before
you know it,' Ben broke in.

'What about you?' Lynne found herself oddly reluctant to withdraw her hand.

He stifled a yawn. 'I'll do a final tour of the wards,
have a hot bath, and there just might be time over for
forty winks. Thanks, Lynne—thanks for everything,'
and Ben took his hand away and lighted a cigarette, but
Lynne saw that some of the despair had left his face.

Monday morning started slowly, to Lynne's relief, as if
the people in the neighbourhood had been shocked by
the grim reality of the coach crash into realising that
their own troubles were very minor indeed. There were
a couple of reporters hanging about the main hospital
entrance, but Lynne kept well out of their way. She
wanted no link, however casual, between last night's
tragedy and the events of the tunnel. How long ago that
seemed, and how unreal. She remembered the mysterious phone call that had preceded their recall to duty.
She was idly curious just enough to wonder if it had
indeed been the Sarah of Timothy Layton's delirium
showing belated concern. She kept watching the door
until she realised with a shock that she was actually
watching it for Ben. No wonder Barbara Stanwell had
looked her way several times before departing with a
pile of X-rays for Records.

Lynne gave herself a little shake. Of course dear Bibs
would have collected all the news about last night. She
might have been pleased to miss all the extra work, but
she certainly would be jealous of being left out of the
drama and excitement. With a pang Lynne remembered
young Shirley's despair. That had been the drama of
tragedy and the only excitement had been threatened
heartbreak. She would call round that way when she
went for her elevenses. Sister Casualty was on duty just
as usual, but she had been summoned to an emergency
meeting of the Admin. Staff. Of course a major alert
meant extra reports, recommendations for future dis-
asters, reprimands for any mishandling—

Lynne heard voices outside the Casualty Theatre
door. No doubt one of the juniors would let her know if
she were wanted.

'It's all right, Nurse. You can count me as staff,' a
voice said coolly.

Lynne looked up to see a tall slim red-headed woman regarding her with an amused smile from the doorway.

'Timothy was right. You *have* got red hair just like mine!'

# CHAPTER SIX

LYNNE could only stare at the smartly dressed stranger. True, they were both red-headed, but Lynne was too honest to imagine that she had anything else in common with the extremely attractive woman who was surveying her with an attention that was too thorough to be reassuring.

'Well, Staff Nurse Howard, is there somewhere we can have a private word?'

Too nonplussed to resist, Lynne led the way to Sister Casualty's office. The other woman sat on the edge of the desk and suggested coolly:

'Shut the door, Staff Nurse. I should imagine there has been enough publicity about this little affair already. Now, suppose you tell me where you're hiding Timothy?'

Anger was beginning to fret at the edges of Lynne's stupefaction. 'I'm not hiding him, and I don't know where he is,' she retorted crisply. She and Ben might have an idea of Timothy Layton's whereabouts, but suspicion wasn't the same as knowing.

The red-headed woman's eyes hardened. 'Stop lying to me, girl. I know all about what went on in that side ward on Neuro Block. A certain junior night nurse was most informative!'

Lynne flushed. 'Information from juniors is not necessarily accurate. Dr Layton was a very sick man!'

'Indeed! Then perhaps you'll tell me why you took it upon yourself to remove him from a place where he was under specialist surveillance!'

Lynne took a deep breath. 'I assure you that I had nothing at all to do with it. I was as surprised as you were!' she added without taking thought.

'But the nurse distinctly said it was your godmother who came for Dr Layton, so you must know about it.'

'I don't—at least not from Aunt Jenny,' Lynne stumbled a little over the words. She didn't know quite what to do. It was one thing for Timothy Layton to rave about a red-headed Sarah, but this red-headed woman didn't *have* to be the same person. It did seem likely that she was, from the evidence of the phone call last night. 'I don't even know who you are,' she said slowly. 'If Dr Layton had wanted his friends notified surely he would have done so.'

'Stop trying to be clever,' the other woman sneered. 'You've already admitted how ill he was. I'm Sarah Wishart—Dr Sarah Wishart, and I'm an old friend of Timothy's—a very good friend,' she added emphatically, watching Lynne's face closely. 'You don't seem altogether surprised. Does that mean Timothy has told you about me?' Some emotion seemed to make her features seem sharper.

'Only that you were called Sarah and that you had red hair, and—' abruptly Lynne stopped short. She had been about to betray a patient's confidence—a revelation that he never knew he had made.

'And?' Sarah Wishart demanded.

But Lynne was wary now. 'Oh, it was all a jumble—they'd given him a sedative, you see.'

Suddenly the arrogance seemed to go out of the other woman. She got down from the desk. 'I wish I knew whether you were telling me the truth. Timothy didn't say where he was staying, just that he was all right and there was no need for me to worry! Just like a man when I'd come all the way down from Scotland when I heard of the accident.' She seemed to be talking half to herself and Lynne wondered if it were an attempt to take her off guard.

She didn't know quite what to do for the best. 'Perhaps if you phone him again Dr Layton may feel more like visitors, Dr Wishart,' Lynne said gently.

'What do you know about phone calls?' the other demanded.

'You did say you hadn't seen Dr Layton, so I thought you'd been talking to him,' Lynne suggested smoothly.

'I'm obviously wasting my time with you, young lady, but don't for the moment think that this is the end of the matter.' Dr Sarah Wishart opened the door, but halfway through she turned back. 'Are you engaged to Timothy?'

But Lynne was beyond pitying her. She simply held out her left hand. 'If you mean am I wearing Timothy's ring? Look for yourself.'

There was a sound of heavy footsteps and Ben Gresham loomed up behind Sarah Wishart. He whistled. 'Well, what have we here? Gemini?'

But Sarah Wishart brushed rudely past him without a word and the click of her heels on the tiled floor had died away before Ben spoke:

'I take it that's the mysterious Sarah?'

Lynne nodded. For a moment she wondered how much Ben had overheard of that final exchange between Sarah Wishart and herself. She still couldn't understand why she had done it.

'No wonder old Timothy confused the two of you the night he was off his head. I suppose he must have told her. I wonder if they'll make it up now that they've met again. I must remember to ask Browning the next time I'm over at Research if he knows what broke them up.'

Lynne let Ben ramble on. Her own thoughts were emotional chaos.

Ben noticed Lynne's silence. 'They *have* met, haven't they?' He guessed the truth from her expression. 'Listen, little one, if you're playing some sort of clever game better let your Uncle Ben know. Otherwise I might drop you in it accidentally.'

Lynne explained as briefly as she could. 'You see, if Timothy wanted to see her he would have told her where he was.'

'Are you letting your Aunt Jenny have first go?' Ben asked shrewdly.

Lynne flushed angrily. 'Of course not! Timothy Layton's a grown man and old enough to run his own life!'

'And his love affairs, eh? Sure you're not the tiniest bit jealous?'

Lynne slowly shook her head, wondering whether she was being strictly truthful. Life had been getting more and more involved ever since that emergency turnout for the tunnel cave-in. The future no longer seemed a smooth and steady climb to her takeover of Sister Casualty's post. Perhaps Aunt Jenny's suggestion of a trip abroad had been unsettling as well.

'Penny for them?'

Lynne had to smile. 'They'd be cheap at a farthing, they're so muddled.'

'Not legal tender. Never mind. What I really came to tell you was that Mr Reynolds operated on Shirley last night—or rather first thing this morning after he'd finished the other cases. He's done a beautiful job. I don't think she'll even have a crooked smile!'

Lynne remembered the girl's anguish. 'I'm so glad,' she said simply. 'Her boy-friend should be pleased.'

'He is, and I had to promise him things wouldn't

change if he went home and got some sleep!' Ben's eyes had a faraway expression and Lynne wondered if he had remembered that little scene in the doctors' changing room. Then he turned and looked at Lynne squarely. 'Thanks for your help, little one. It isn't often that your Uncle Ben lets the rest of the world see what a softie he can be.'

'I'm not the rest of the world,' Lynne reminded him gently.

'Thank God for that! He patted Lynne's shoulder and for a moment his hand lingered.

A sharp tap at the door and then Barbara Stanwell's over-sweet tones interrupted them: 'So sorry, I thought Sister was back. Your lights are on, Dr Gresham. There's an ambulance drawing up, Staff Nurse. Shall I see to it?'

'Yes, please do, Staff Nurse,' Lynne told the girl, simply to get rid of her. Normally it was her own task to receive any cases and then assign them according to their injuries and the duty rota.

Ben was on the phone. 'Yes, I'll be right up.' He turned back to Lynne. 'Be seeing you. I'll be on Men's Surgical if you need me for the new case.'

Lynne guessed he wanted to get away, and she couldn't blame him. Dear Bibs had managed with her usual success to spoil things, to add a nasty flavour to something that had been simple and nice. 'All right, Ben, and thank you for telling me about Shirley. I was going to see her when I went for my elevenses.'

'You do just that. She'll have to lie pretty still for the next few days, and life could get a bit boring.'

The phone rang and by the time Lynne had dealt with the enquiry Ben had gone. Lynne went to see how Barbara Stanwell was getting on.

The girl looked up as Lynne came into the dressing

room. 'Only an injured finger, Staff Nurse. I can manage.'

Lynne saw the young workman sitting on the stool and noticed how attentively he was surveying the girl's trim figure, and hid a smile. No wonder dear Bibs was sure she could manage!

Sister Casualty beckoned to Lynne from the doorway and together they went into the office.

'Sorry to be so long, Staff Nurse. Any other cases?'

'No, Sister.' Lynne stood politely at attention in front of the desk. She knew the older woman would tell her about the meeting in her own time and in her own way.

'Sit down, Staff Nurse. In case you haven't guessed it already we've been highly commended for our work last night. Don't get too conceited if I tell you that you came in for special praise.'

Lynne flushed. 'Thank you for telling me, Sister, but the two juniors were wonderful, and Dr Gresham, of course.'

Sister Casualty chuckled. 'I know. We all were—it's official. You'd better go to elevenses and take one of the juniors with you. It looks like being a quiet morning for a change. You needn't come back until five. You've earned yourself some extra time off.'

Lynne didn't waste time protesting that she wasn't the only one. When Sister Casualty used that firm tone no one argued. Suddenly it was a wonderful morning and the harrowing scenes of last night were already fading fast. She would get on a bus and ride out to the open country, or she would find a green park and walk and walk. The thought of Sarah Wishart flickered across her mind, but not even that mystery could hold her attention for long.

By the time Lynne had changed out of uniform a few tiny clouds were breaking up the clear expanse of blue sky. She decided that a walk in a green park would be the better bargain. As she swung on to the bus she noticed a small white car starting up on the far side of the road. The driver appeared to be in no hurry to get anywhere, content to idle along a few hundred yards behind the bus. Lynne was envious for a moment before deciding that it must be some busy mother with a little time to spare before collecting a school child for lunch.

The park was almost empty apart from the groups of prams parked round the benches fortunate enough to be in the sun. Here and there an old man sat and read his paper thankful that it was warm enough to be away from some lonely room. Lynne walked at a brisk pace at first, unable to appreciate that she had time on her hands for a change. As she neared the duckpond she slowed down, happy to watch the four-year-olds clutching large crusts that they broke into small pieces to throw with excited little cries to the ducks clamouring rudely for more.

Lynne slipped her mac off and used it for a cushion on top of a convenient wall. The sun was pleasantly warm and it was pleasant to have no duties demanding her attention. The sharp click of heels on the concrete path roused her, but when she turned round there was only the glimpse of someone's back disappearing round a clump of shrubs. Someone in a hurry, someone with no time to notice the sunshine. Lynne watched the young mothers chatting in the sun and for a moment she envied them. They had homes and husbands and children and time to sit. Her own life seemed an empty sham, and then she remembered young Shirley and the smile on the youthful face.

'You and that doctor were right, Nurse. Mr Reynolds says I won't know it ever happened in a few weeks. Thanks for coming to see me. My boy will be back in a bit when he's had some sleep.'

Well, perhaps some of her life had meaning. Lynne stood up and gave herself a little shake. A cup of tea in the park café would sort her gloomy thoughts. The café was more crowded than Lynne had expected. A number of office girls taking an early lunch and tempted by the sunshine sat at the tables by the windows. Lynne had to be content with one on the far side of the entrance. The tea was hot and strong and the ham sandwiches tastier than she expected. Lynne sat back and watched the people coming and going—no one she really recognised, but a few faces that seemed familiar. That was one drawback of working in Casualty—so many people passing through but never time to get to know any of them. Of course it wasn't all tragedies. Often there were near miracles or joyous reunions particularly after major incidents. It had to be like that or not even devoted people like Sister Casualty would have stuck to it until retiring age.

Lynne's attention was drawn to someone who had come in with a crowd of giggling girls, and then she smiled to herself. How silly to think that there were only a few red-heads out and about this glorious morning and that they had to be someone she knew or had met. She was being silly, and she certainly had no real reason to take the reappearance of Sarah Wishart in Timothy Layton's life as part of her concern. It seemed even more stupid to wish that she and the Senior Casualty Officer were back on their former hostile footing. At least there had been no emotional involvement then, unless angry irritation came under that heading.

Lynne paid for her snack lunch and headed for the path that ran round the perimeter of the park. She would take the long way to the bus stop as a sort of penance for being upset by silly encounters with people that had nothing to do with her. She walked briskly and refused to be tempted into lingering this time. She had to run the last few yards to catch the bus.

The driver grinned as he gave her a ticket. 'Good thing I recognised you, Nurse, from when you fixed up Jimmy's foot. Got a morning off, eh? Me and the missus often talks about you and St David's. Not like some I could name, you took the time to tell us what was what and that he'd be all right. You should see him now—the best runner in his class. Suppose you're on your way back. Read all about you in the Sunday papers. The missus saw you on TV and recognised that red mop of yours—begging your pardon, Nurse, but it was lucky for that poor bloke as well as for our Jimmy.' He chuckled at Lynne's blushes and started up the bus.

She sat down quickly in a front seat and hoped not too many of the passengers had overheard. It was nice to be appreciated, but not quite so publicly. Lynne looked out of the window watching the houses whizz by and envied the people who could potter in their gardens, the thin swirls of smoke rising from bonfires as they tidied up ready for winter. Ben had been right. Hospital staff really did live apart from the world. Idly she saw a small white car swing out to pass the bus. Of course there were plenty of small white cars in a big city and she hadn't bothered to notice the number plate on the one she had noticed earlier.

For no reason at all Lynne got off the bus a stop sooner than usual. The driver gave her a puzzled but friendly grin as he drove on. She would drop in on Aunt Jenny and thank her for the party. After all, she and Ben had had to leave in a hurry. Some instinct made her decide to turn off and take the service road which ran behind the row of big houses. Many like Aunt Jenny's had been converted into flats, but they still possessed large gardens at the rear.

As Lynne went through the garden gate she could see someone sitting in one of the big chairs her godmother kept on the stone-paved patio. It wasn't until she was almost up to the garden seat that Lynne realised it wasn't her godmother sitting there but Timothy Layton. His eyes were closed and his face looked thinner than she remembered, but his cheeks were flushed from the sun and he had lost that harassed expression. She was about to tiptoe away in embarrassment when his eyes opened.

'Wait, Lynne—please wait.'

Reluctantly she came back. 'I was looking for my godmother, Dr Layton,' she explained rather stiffly.

'Mrs Leslie has taken the Darrells to the clinic—it's the day for their feet. I'm not expecting them back before five. Won't you sit down? I've been wanting to thank you for—' it was his turn to appear embarrassed. 'I don't remember very much, but Night Sister did say how helpful you'd been. I'm afraid I may have upset you by some of the things I said. Believe me, it was the last thing I would have wanted. It was silly of me to mix you up with Sarah—'

It was Lynne who broke in hastily, 'It's all right, Dr Layton. I was only too glad to help. I realise that you and Dr Wishart are old friends and—'

Timothy Layton sat up abruptly. 'You mean you and Sarah have met? Good God, does that mean she knows where I am?'

Lynne was startled by his agitation. 'You mean you don't *want* to see her again? I thought—'

Before he could answer there was a loud peal of the front doorbell. Lynne started to move towards the open back door, but Timothy Layton held up a hand to stop her.

'Leave it. There's no one expected, and it could be—'

'You mean Dr Wishart?'

He nodded. 'She said she wouldn't give up until she found me. I told her it was all over and that she was wasting her time.'

'Has Dr Wishart got a white car?' Lynne wished the question didn't sound so irrelevant.

'Quite possibly—she always liked smart things,' Timothy Layton's tone was irritable. 'I suppose she implied that there was a romantic attachment?'

Lynne flushed a little. 'Perhaps, but it was what you said—' she stopped in acute embarrassment.

'It's all right, Lynne. I admit I was at one time very much in love with Sarah Wishart, but she chose someone else. I suppose I buried it all too deep under my work and it took a silly knock on the head to bring it up to the surface. Suppose we have a cup of tea and forget about the whole sorry business? Mrs Darrell left the tray ready if you'd like to plug the electric kettle in.'

Lynne and Timothy were finishing their second cups when they heard someone give a little cough. Startled, they looked up to see Jenny Leslie standing at the edge of the patio.

'What on earth are you doing here, Lynne?' Her tone was more unfriendly than Lynne had ever remembered.

'Dodging unwelcome visitors and keeping me company until you and the Darrells got back. I didn't expect you so soon, Jenny,' Timothy Layton interposed smoothly.

'The shops were crowded, so I thought I would come back here until it was time to collect the Darrells from the clinic, that's all. What's this about visitors?' Her voice was calmer now.

It was Lynne who rushed in impulsively with an explanation. 'We thought it might be Sarah Wishart, so—' Too late she saw Timothy Layton's warning gesture. Aghast, she watched Jenny Leslie's face go white and then flush with anger.

'That damned woman! How many more men does she want?' She turned on her heel and walked hurriedly away with the unsteady steps of somebody who wasn't seeing clearly because her eyes were full of tears.

A door had slammed in the distance before Lynne ventured to break the uneasy silence. 'What on earth have I done?'

Timothy Layton shrugged his shoulders. 'I don't suppose it's your fault. I didn't know how much you knew. I said Sarah went off with someone. She did—with John Leslie.'

'But I thought he was dead—though Mother never really said—' Lynne was beginning to feel more bewildered every moment.

'He is,' Timothy Layton's tone was grim. 'There was a car crash, but no one really knew who was driving, Sarah or John. She was badly injured—there was talk of amnesia. I don't remember the outcome of the enquiry. I'd changed my job by then and simply didn't want to know. When Jenny turned up on Neuro with her invitation naturally we didn't discuss John's death. Possibly she didn't even know that Sarah and I had been friends. Most of the university crowd had pretty casual relationships and I suppose I felt more strongly about Sarah than she did about me—I don't know. I suppose it would have come out in time. I'm only sorry that it happened like this. Jenny has had enough hurt as it is.'

Lynne stood up. 'I think I'd better go. I don't know how I'm going to face Aunt Jenny after this.'

'Leave it for a few days. I'll try to sort things out—if she'll let me. Thanks again for your help.'

'It was an odd kind of help,' Lynne said a little bitterly. 'However, I didn't give Dr Wishart your address. After all, we don't know that it was her at the door, and there are lots of white cars—if she has got one.' She remembered her impression in the park that she was being followed, but it seemed silly to mention it now. 'Thanks for the tea. I have to be on duty by five.'

Timothy Layton's face was a trifle wistful. 'I wish I was back on duty, but the big shots say another week. I can give my lecture at the school—they think talking about safety won't excite me too much. I'll see you next week if not before.'

Lynne took a back way to the nurses' home. She had upset enough people for one day.

Sister Casualty was at tea and Barbara Stanwell and Ben Gresham were dealing with a casualty in the plaster room. The sound of gay laughter and light-hearted chatter suggested that dear Bibs wouldn't be at all pleased if Lynne offered to relieve her. So Lynne contented herself with giving the junior on duty a hand.

The girl heaved a sigh of relief. 'Thank goodness you're back, Staff Nurse. Sister had a message from Matron at four-thirty and those two in the plaster room have been there for simply ages. I managed the dressings all right. They were easy ones and the kiddies were as good as gold. I've put the details down in the book and their mum's having a cup of tea. I didn't know quite what to do, in case they should have a shot of anti-tetanus.'

Lynne reassured her. 'Better go for your tea. I'll have a word with Dr Gresham. Were they clean lacerations?'

'They were clean enough, but the kiddies' knees were on the dirty side. Their mum said someone had been knocking over milk bottles. Luckily the pieces of glass must have been pretty small.'

Lynne heard the slam of the plaster room door. 'I'll catch Dr Gresham. Off you go, Nurse.'

There was no sign of Barbara Stanwell. Perhaps she just might be clearing up before she went off duty.

'Dr Gresham!' Lynne realised she was being more formal than usual.

Ben Gresham swung round. 'Yes, Staff Nurse?' His tone was curt, but Lynne didn't pay too much attention.

'Do you want these two youngsters to have a shot before they go?'

Ben glanced across at the little group near the tea urn. 'You must be joking, Staff Nurse! The Smith twins won't need a topping-up shot for another six months! If they don't turn up once a fortnight in Casualty I begin to think they must have moved away!'

Lynne flushed. It was her own fault for not checking the casualty record book. 'Sorry, I didn't realise it was the "terrible twins". Are you finished in the plaster room?'

Ben shrugged his shoulders. 'As far as I know. Bibs has taken the youngster down to X-Ray for a follow-on plate. Now, if you'll excuse me, Grant is standing in for me for three hours. Shout for him if you want anything, won't you?'

He walked away leaving Lynne staring after him. Never in all the time she had known him had she been treated quite so distantly. What on earth was the matter with him? No doubt someone or something had upset him. She told Mrs Smith it was all right to take the children home.

'Better bring them back tomorrow, Mrs Smith. We can check the dressings then.'

'Ta ever so, Nurse. You'll be lucky if they keeps the dressings on that long. Come on, you two, and stop being cheeky!'

Lynne stifled a sigh and went to deal with the plaster room. She wondered if Barbara Stanwell was waiting in X-Ray with the fracture case. The worst of the mess was out of the way by the time the junior staff nurse appeared in the doorway.

'Thanks a lot, Staff Nurse. I didn't know I'd be so long in X-Ray. The child has been admitted and the mother's gone up with him to the ward.' She hesitated a moment. 'Has Dr Gresham gone, then?'

There was something that suggested triumph in the way the girl put the question. It made Lynne pick up the plaster bowl and walk across to the sink before answering.

'Yes, he's gone out for the next three hours, I believe.'

There was no mistaking the gloating now. 'Good—I must get changed. He doesn't like being kept waiting, does he? I've left the list on Sister's desk—I don't know if she's coming back to the department.' The younger girl turned to go. 'And thanks for clearing up. Have fun!'

Lynne didn't answer. She was too angry not to show it if she had faced her junior. The cheek of her! It took several moments of hard cleaning before Lynne had simmered down. After all, dear Bibs and Ben Gresham had enjoyed one another's company in the past. It was only because Timothy Layton was on sick leave that the usual routines had been all topsy-turvy. It depended upon the duty rotas, but usually the senior staff nurse looked after the Senior Casualty Officer and the junior staff nurse took the Junior Casualty Officer's cases—at least up until five o'clock. After that it depended upon who was on call.

Lynne heard Sister Casualty's slow footsteps coming across the Casualty Hall and went out to meet her. How tired the older woman looked! Lynne wondered whether anything upsetting had happened after she had gone off.

'Oh, there you are, Staff Nurse. Come along to the office if you're finished.'

Lynne followed her senior. Sister Casualty would tell

her if something was wrong, but the older woman didn't like questions from anyone.

'Sit down and close the door, there's a good girl. We'll hear the bell if there's a case.'

Lynne obeyed. This sounded serious.

'I've been with Matron for the last three-quarters of an hour. It hasn't been exactly pleasant and I still don't know the answer.' She looked sharply at Lynne. 'It wasn't entirely about you, but too much so for my liking. Remember that case last night—the facial lacerations? Well, who suggested that Mr Reynolds should attend to her last night?'

Lynne was silent from sheer astonishment and then finally found her voice. 'I suppose it must have been arranged by Dr Gresham. I didn't know anything about it until he told me this morning.'

The older woman heaved a sigh of relief. 'Thank goodness for that! Now, another thing, did you have a visitor this morning before you went off—and I don't mean a patient?'

Lynne thought back hastily. 'If you mean Dr Wishart, she was looking for Dr Layton and wanted to know where he was. Someone on Neuro had told her I would know.'

'And did you tell her?'

'No, Sister—I wasn't sure then.'

The older woman nodded. 'Dr Wishart must have gone to Matron after she left Casualty. Fortunately Matron had someone waiting to see her, so she could only spare a few minutes for Dr Wishart. It was long enough for that young woman to cause Matron some misgivings. As a result I had a second meeting with Matron, and I assure you it wasn't all bouquets of praise this time. I don't know whether you're aware of it or not, but at least one person appears to have a grudge against you, and I'm not entirely satisfied that someone in this department isn't involved.'

Lynne flushed and moved uneasily. Once she might have included Timothy Layton among those hostile to her promised promotion, but at least he was eliminated now. That left dear Bibs, and surely a few clashes of personality didn't add up to a grudge—or did it?

'It's all right, Staff Nurse. I don't expect you to tell me—if you do happen to know. I merely want you to be on your guard. I don't want to retire, but at least I'll go more happily if the transfer of responsibility is a smooth one. I made it plain to Matron that I was quite happy about handing over to you when the time comes. Let's try to keep it that way.'

'I'll do my best,' Lynne promised fervently, 'and thank you for standing up for me, Sister.'

'Perhaps I was only looking after my own interests,' the older woman said dryly, but Lynne was pleased to see her superior looked more relaxed. 'I'll be off now, and I trust you'll have a peaceful afternoon.'

Lynne escorted Sister Casualty to the door of the department and kept her fingers crossed all the way back to the office. With Ben Gresham 'out' until five o'clock and only a house surgeon standing in for him anything could happen.

Her particular magic couldn't have been working very well. The break in the calm of the afternoon came while Lynne was at tea. She was called to the phone and she knew from the shake in the junior's voice that there was real trouble down in Casualty.

'Staff Nurse, can you come quickly? Matron and Mr Reynolds are here and two ambulances are on their way—a lorry went through the plate glass window at the supermarket. We can't find Dr Gresham anywhere!'

'Steady on—get out the emergency plastic drums and

switch on the sterilisers in the casualty theatre and the dressing rooms. I'll collect Dr Grant on my way down.'

Lynne heard the younger girl's sigh of relief as a little of the tension went out of her voice. She wished she felt as confident herself. If only Ben had been more specific! She didn't know whether he had asked the Senior Registrar for permission or whether it had been a private arrangement with Grant. She would have to tread carefully and cover up for Ben if need be. She ignored the tiny core of anger still lingering from dear Bibs' triumphant announcement of her date with Ben.

The sound of upraised voices as Lynne turned the corner of the corridor leading to Casualty warned Lynne that her instinct about trouble was only too true. She glanced back at Peter Grant.

'I hope Ben's excuse is a good one,' she whispered, and then setting her shoulders she marched forward to deal with the situation.

# CHAPTER SEVEN

'SISTER Casualty, I am not saying that it is *your* fault that we're trying to cope with this situation without a casualty officer. I'm merely suggesting that it isn't good enough. I know you are off duty and I'm sure not even Matron would have called you back.' Mr Reynolds' tone held exasperated sorrow rather than anger.

Lynne would have given anything not to have continued towards the little group. It didn't take Peter Grant's deep sigh behind her to warn her that he was as reluctant as she.

'Staff Nurse! Where on earth have you been all this time?' Matron's voice held pent-up irritation and Lynne knew she must tread delicately.

'I was collecting Dr Grant who is standing in for Dr Gresham, Matron. I thought it would save time. I'll get Casualty Theatre ready right away, Mr Reynolds.' She began to edge away towards the theatre door.

'Not so fast, young lady,' Mr Reynolds broke in. 'Surely you know where Dr Gresham is? He has no business being out of the department at this time of day. He should take his off duty at the proper time like anyone else.'

Lynne's self-control snapped abruptly. 'Mr Reynolds, I don't think you realise that with Dr Layton off ill, Dr Gresham has had no proper off duty at *any* time. If it hadn't been for Dr Grant's kindness he still would be on call round the clock!' It didn't take the icy silence to tell Lynne she had overstepped every possible boundary. Only the clang of the bell from the approaching ambulance staved off the inevitable.

'Staff Nurse, you and Dr Grant take Casualty Theatre. We'll send the patients in to you after we've sorted out the more serious ones for admission.' Sister Casualty's tone was bleaker than Lynne ever remembered, and she walked away quickly with Peter Grant trailing at her heels.

As Lynne paused in the doorway to let the house surgeon go first she heard Sister Casualty saying briefly to Matron, 'Thank you for coming down, Matron. We'll be all right now.'

'Whew! You certainly did your best to save old Ben's bacon,' Peter Grant said admiringly as he slipped on the gown Lynne held out for him.

'I've probably grilled my own instead,' Lynne sighed. 'The people at the top never bother to enquire how we're managing to cope until it's too late. If Ben hadn't been tough he would have cracked up long ago.'

'Nonsense, Lynne! Your Uncle Ben isn't a softie.'

Lynne and the house surgeon turned and gaped at Ben Gresham in the doorway. He already had a gown on, a mask was hanging round his neck, and he was carrying a small girl wearing a bloodstained handkerchief round her head.

'Just a small gash—if you trim back the hair and use a spray-on dressing. All right, Lucy, if I leave you with Uncle Peter?'

The child nodded tearfully. 'You will look for my dolly, Uncle Ben, and tell Mummy not to be too long?'

'Course I will,' Ben promised. As he handed over the child he made a gesture that warned them that Lucy's mother was among the more serious casualties that were being admitted.

Lynne found a dolly for Lucy and handed the child over to one of the waiting relatives in the Casualty Hall, then went back to help Peter Grant with the next case. It seemed for a time that the string of patients would never end. They dressed cuts, bandaged knees and ankles damaged in the panic rush following the crash. Two of the volunteers came back to make tea for the waiting throng, hearing on the invisible grapevine about the accident. There were police and reporters. There were relatives waiting stony-faced for news from the main theatres where Mr Reynolds and another surgeon were working flat out to repair the damage.

'They say the driver had a heart attack, fell across the wheel, but nobody knows whether it happened before it happened or because it was going to happen,' a young reporter told Lynne gravely.

Lynne hurried away, only too thankful that he hadn't recognized her, but her relief didn't last for long. As she bent down to pick up another child there was the hurting glare of a flashbulb and a photographer grumbling softly,

'Wish the papers went in for colour, Staff Nurse!'

But Lynne was too busy hushing the child to care. She found that Ben had taken over from Peter Grant.

'The wards were shouting for him. I think we can manage now. There are only a couple of women left— they said they didn't mind waiting. I have a sneaking suspicion they're half enjoying all the excitement now that the worst is over. Luckily no one was killed, except for the driver.'

Lynne sat the little boy on the edge of the theatre table. 'They said he had a heart attack. Ben, how come you got back so quickly? I thought you said you were out for three hours—' she stopped abruptly, remembering the circumstances under which they had parted. She wondered where dear Bibs had got to.

Ben looked a trifle sheepish. 'I was only across the way

and when I saw the two ambulances drawing up I came back,' he said simply. 'I left Bibs to her steak and chips. I don't know how the girl manages to keep such a slim figure with the food she puts away. Well, young man, what can we do for you?'

'It's only a little bloody—it's my mummy I want. I don't know where they tooked her when she fell down.'

Lynne picked up a swab and began to wipe away the blood from the small arm to reveal a minute scratch. She exchanged looks with Ben. No doubt in all the rush and panic the child had been bundled in with the rest into the ambulances. His mother might have fainted or been trampled.

'What's your name, sonny?' Ben put a large strip of plaster over the tiny cut and winked at Lynne.

'It's Ben Gardiner, and I'm six years old and I live with Mummy and Daddy at my grandmother's house, ten Grevelin Terrace. Do you know where that is?' the child demanded suddenly.

'We can always ask a policeman,' Ben reassured him.

'Lynne, how about popping out and asking Sister Casualty about Mrs Gardiner? You can send one of those two women in. I can be dealing with her injuries while we're waiting.'

Lynne went reluctantly. For the first time she had a moment to think about the consequences of her outburst, and she was dreading the first encounter.

Sister Casualty gave no sign of remembering. 'Mrs Gardiner? There's no one of that name been admitted. Better ask some of the people still waiting for transport. Someone might know.'

Lynne heaved a sigh of relief. Perhaps only Matron and Mr Reynolds were going to hold it against her. As she went out into the main Casualty hall she heard a commotion near the ambulance entrance. A young woman was trying to tell one of the policemen something, but she was sobbing too loudly to make much sense.

'Steady on, missus, maybe the nurse knows. She says her little boy must be here—they told her he was in the ambulance.'

Lynne went over to the frantic mother. 'If his name is Ben and he's six years old and lives at ten Grevelin Terrace,' she began, but before she could finish the woman pulled fiercely at her arm.

'Is he very badly hurt, Nurse? Tell me quickly!'

'Just a very tiny cut, Mrs Gardiner. I think he must have got someone else's blood on him, so they thought he was worse than he was. Would you like to come this way?'

Ben was busy bandaging a cut elbow for the woman Lynne had sent in to him, but it was *young* Ben who was holding the floor.

'We live with Gran and Granddad because Mummy works too. Everything costs so much, even my pocket money. One day we're going to live in the country when we've saved enough. I'm saving up too, for a puppy— it'll be better in the country for him and—' then he saw his mother and scrambled down from his stool. 'Are you all picked up now, Mummy? Can we go home and have tea? I'm ever so hungry and they don't seem to have tea in this place. The doctor's name is Ben, too.'

The young mother's eyes widened as she saw the large strip of plaster on her son's arm.

Ben Gresham smiled at her. 'For snob reasons only, I promise you, Mrs Gardiner.'

Then she began to laugh, although tears weren't far away. 'He scratched his arm before we went out,' she explained.

Ben and Lynne exchanged grins.

'Never mind, it's all part of the service at St David's,' Ben said generously.

'Then how about seeing to me, young man?' a voice demanded from the doorway—the last of their casualties had become impatient.

There was almost an air of gaiety about the Casualty theatre as Ben and Lynne completed the last dressing. The ambulances had returned to collect the remaining cases and the big Casualty hall was empty at last, only a final wisp of steam curled up from the tea urn to prove that the department had indeed been as busy as any rush hour.

Ben sat on the edge of the theatre table and watched Lynne clear away the final traces of their work.

'Thanks for sticking up for me, Lynne. I didn't get a chance before.'

Lynne flushed. 'I didn't know you knew,' she said a trifle stiffly.

'I happened to overhear most of it. You should have seen old Reynolds' face!'

'I was too angry to notice. I suppose Matron and Sister Casualty were looking daggers too.' Lynne was beginning to feel embarrassed.

'I think they were too stunned by your audacity!' Ben chuckled.

'Well, it was true. You haven't had any proper off-duty—it's not fair.'

'If you two have finished arguing I suggest you go to supper, Staff Nurse,' said Sister Casualty tartly from the doorway. 'Then perhaps I can resume *my* proper off-duty!'

Ben Gresham slid to his feet. 'Sister Casualty, I trust that the powers-to-be aren't going to penalise Staff Nurse for what she said.'

The older woman smiled a trifle grimly. 'I think that

you can leave the matter safely in my hands, Dr Gresham. Actually I had already suggested to the Committee that you were being dangerously overworked.'

'Whew! Thanks, Sister. I didn't know I had such a champion.'

'Not just you, young man. Now suppose you take yourself off and perhaps we'll have a little normality round here!'

Ben agreed and smiled cheekily as he obeyed.

'I'm sorry if I embarrassed you, Sister,' Lynne said impulsively.

'It needed saying, Staff Nurse, although I agree that perhaps you weren't the one to say it. Shall we let the matter drop for the time being? The sooner you're back from supper—'

'Sorry, Sister, I didn't mean—'

Casualty Sister gave Lynne a little push, but there was affection rather than impatience in the gesture.

When Lynne got off duty she found a message—a most unexpected one—waiting for her. It was from Dr Timothy Layton asking her to come and see him urgently, by the back entrance. Lynne turned over the envelope curiously. There was no postmark on it. She wondered if he had left it himself or found a messenger. There was no point in trying to find out who had brought it.

Rather reluctantly Lynne changed out of her uniform. Not only was she physically tired, but she felt emotionally drained after the day's events. The thought of being involved for the second time today in Timothy Layton's affairs filled her with dismay. The memory of Aunt Jenny's white tortured face still haunted her and she couldn't be sure that her godmother mightn't interrupt them again.

Timothy Layton opened the door at Lynne's first

hesitant tap. His rather worried expression vanished at the sight of Lynne.

'Come in, Lynne, my dear. I was beginning to be afraid you weren't coming after all.'

Lynne began to explain about the accident, but he cut in, 'It's all right, Lynne. Mr Reynolds was on the phone earlier! You might like to know that the powers-that-be have agreed to let me return to work tomorrow instead of waiting until next week.' He saw Lynne's flush and chuckled. 'I understand I have you to thank, in part, for the reversal of their decision. I wish I had been able to hear it.'

Lynne was too embarrassed to share his amusement. 'You wanted to see me urgently, Dr Layton,' she reminded him.

'So I do. Sit over there and I'll make us a pot of tea. Everything's ready.' He saw Lynne's anxious glance towards the door. 'Don't worry, your godmother is out this evening at a concert. It's about her that I wanted to see you.'

Lynne stared at him in utter astonishment, but he made no attempt to satisfy her until he had made the tea.

'A good cup of nurses' brew should put you right, eh? All right, my dear, I can see you're dying with curiosity. Well, the fact of the matter is that I'll be moving back to my own quarters tomorrow. I'll be doing the night calls for several nights to make up for all young Gresham's overtime, and I can't do that from here. As I was the unfortunate cause of Mrs Leslie's being reminded of her own tragedy I feel very guilty about leaving her completely on her own at such short notice. I know she has her own friends, but I don't believe they're close enough to be of any comfort. So I'm asking you to make a special point of being here for the next few evenings. I only hope it won't interfere too much with any of your own engagements.'

Lynne stared at him aghast. 'But, Dr Layton, I don't think Aunt Jenny will even want to see me—not after what happened today.'

'We had a long talk before she went out this evening. Jenny knows now how you came to be involved, and I'm sure she understands. I think she would enjoy your company, as long as your parents don't know what's happened. You and I are involved, by the sheer chance of Sarah's coming back into the picture, but I'll make sure that no one else is hurt!' He ended with a fierceness that reminded Lynne of the clashes between them when he had first come to Casualty.

Lynne still felt uneasy about Timothy Layton's belief that Aunt Jenny would welcome her company. However, she finally agreed to come over tomorrow after she came off duty at five.

'Don't phone first, just turn up. She's really very fond of you, my dear. Thanks very much for coming over—and remember, not a word to anyone.'

Lynne walked slowly along the service road at the back of the houses. There was a slip of a moon just bright enough to add a glitter to the scatter of frost crystals on the leaves. Lynne shivered a little. Soon it would be winter, and spring seemed a long way off. As she emerged on to the main road Lynne saw someone standing by a nearby lamp-post, walking a dog, most likely.

'Hello, Lynne, been visiting someone?'

Lynne jumped. 'Ben! You startled me. What on earth are you doing here?'

'Are the streets closed to junior casualty officers, then? I might ask you the same. Been to see Aunt Jenny?'

Lynne was about to tell him she hadn't when she saw where the admission might land her. 'I just dropped in and now I'm heading for my bed.' She pretended to hide a yawn.

He hesitated. 'So I can't invite you to have a coffee with me?'

Lynne shook her head. 'Not this time, Ben, if you don't mind. It's been rather a day.'

'You can say that again. OK, little one, Uncle Ben will have to show you his appreciation another day. How about having dinner with me tomorrow? Old Timothy returns to the fold and yours truly will be having some proper off-duty.'

Lynne remembered in time to show surprise. 'I thought he was off for another week. Sorry about tomorrow night. I'll be at Aunt Jenny's.'

Ben peered at her. 'What again, so soon? I knew you were friendly, but—'

'An emergency has come up,' Lynne said hastily, 'and I promised I'd help out. Thanks again, Ben, but I really must have an early night.'

Ben held out a hand to stop her. 'Don't make excuses to your Uncle Ben, Lynne. Surely I deserve better than that! Is something wrong? You can always tell me.'

Lynne hesitated. She had already told Ben the beginning of the story, but somehow it no longer seemed right to cut him in on Timothy Layton's private life. Now that Aunt Jenny was involved the need for secrecy seemed more imperative than ever. Before she could say anything Ben spoke:

'Lynne, there's no real reason why you have to cut yourself off from the world, surely—I didn't realise how few friends you had until Bibs pointed it out. Is it because you're in line for Sister Casualty's post?'

Lynne nearly choked in sheer astonishment. How

dared that wretched girl discuss her behind her back!

'Don't be silly, Ben! Of course it isn't—it just happens that none of my set stayed on at St David's. I see some of them when I'm on holiday. If Bibs wasn't—' she stopped abruptly. Calling the girl a silly little flirt when she had been out with Ben today wasn't quite the thing to say.

'Sorry I spoke. I was only trying to help. Goodnight, Lynne.' Ben turned on his heel and walked rapidly off in the direction of the main hospital block.

For a moment Lynne was tempted to run after him, but she didn't. Somewhere over the past twenty-four hours she had lost contact with their familiar wavelength. Perhaps it was her fault, or Ben's, or dear Bibs', or even Timothy Layton's. True, the appearance of Dr Sarah Wishart could have started off the chain of unhappy events. Lynne sighed and walked slowly up to her room. She would need plenty of sleep to cope with Dr Timothy Layton's first day back on duty. The fact that he had asked for her help tonight didn't guarantee that he would give her an easier time at work.

So much for Lynne's hopes. The day started badly. Bibs upset the juniors by biting their heads off for no apparent fault. Lynne rescued them as discreetly as possible only to have the junior staff nurse walk away muttering.

'What's upset her?' Lynne enquired cautiously.

The girl grinned cheekily. 'Her big date got interrupted, that's why, Staff Nurse. We heard about it and we didn't know she was anywhere near.'

Lynne hid a smile. 'Better be careful next time. You two can do the plaster trolleys. You'll have to get some more three-inch bandages from the storeroom. Here are the keys. Dr Layton is back, and he's a terror for that width.' She saw the surprised looks on their faces and realised that his return wasn't general knowledge. Oh well, it probably wouldn't matter, and no one would wonder where she had got the news.

Sister Casualty called her and Lynne forgot about it. The older woman looked tired.

'I was hoping we'd have a trouble-free day just for once,' Sister Casualty spoke half to herself. Then seeing Lynne's surprise she pulled herself together. 'I don't know why I thought you would have heard. Dr Gresham is laid up with a broken ankle—slipped on an icy pavement, they say. I didn't even know we'd had a frost!' She glanced down at a slip of paper in her hand. 'They've dug up a woman doctor for Casualty from somewhere. I'll have Junior Staff Nurse look after her. You take Dr Layton's cases—all right?'

Lynne sensed the anxiety in her senior's voice. 'Of course, Sister. I left the juniors doing the plaster trolleys.'

'Good girl—if there really is ice on the pavements we'll be needing all the three-inch plaster bandages we have!'

Lynne smiled. 'I've already sent for more, Sister.'

She left the office and hurried towards the plaster room. *When* and *how* had Ben managed to break an ankle? He had certainly been all right when she had seen him, and cold sober, of that she was convinced. Surely her refusal to have dinner with him tonight wouldn't have prompted him to go off the deep end? It was all so silly—if only she hadn't promised Timothy Layton to look after Aunt Jenny and probably her godmother wouldn't be at all pleased. It was all such a muddle.

'Staff Nurse, I'm ready for the first case *when* you are,' Dr Timothy Layton's crisp tone cut into Lynne's thoughts.

Lynne flushed and gestured to the junior nurse to push the plaster trolley closer. She hadn't heard him come in.

Casualty Sister had been right. It seemed that every-one in the immediate vicinity of St David's had slipped on the first icy pavements of the years. An endless procession of ankles, wrists, bruised ribs, disjointed thumbs, kept them busy—through the coffee break, through the lunch hour, until Sister Casualty's tart voice:

'Staff Nurse, why didn't you send one of your juniors to first lunch?'

Lynne straightened her aching back and gave a final smoothing touch to the plaster cast on a young lad's leg.

'Sorry, Sister, I hadn't realised it was so late.'

'My fault, Sister,' Timothy Layton put in quietly. 'I was trying to clear the bench before the afternoon batch turned up.'

Casualty Sister smiled wearily. 'And what will you use for staff if my nurses are all at late lunch? Never mind, I'll send one of the other juniors in to clear away. Junior Staff and Dr Wishart have finished their list and—'

Even Sister Casualty must have sensed the sudden chill silence that had fallen over the little group round the plaster table by now, Lynne thought dully. She was almost afraid to look in Timothy Layton's direction.

It was he who found his voice first. 'Did you say Dr Wishart, Sister?' his tone suggesting disbelief, almost contempt for what he had heard.

'Yes, Dr Layton, a red-headed woman—very efficient, I should think. It appears that she was re-sponsible for Dr Gresham's accident and felt she should volunteer to help us out, in the circumstances.'

'She would,' but perhaps only Lynne sensed the bitterness behind the quiet comment.

Sister Casualty helped their patient down from the table. 'Try hopping as far as the bench, young man. Off you go to lunch, Staff Nurse, and take the two juniors with you. Dr Layton, I suggest you go for yours as well.

You're looking a trifle peaky—are you sure you're really fit for work?'

Lynne slipped away with the two juniors. There was nothing she could do to help Timothy Layton at this point. To think that Ben Gresham was responsible for crashing down the safety barriers she had erected so carefully to protect a sick man from his unhappy past. Just wait until she had time for a few strong words with Ben Gresham!

Lynne came down the steps from the canteen and the girl at the reception desk held out a hand to stop her rushing past.

'Staff Nurse, I've a message for you from Dr Gresham. He'd like to see you—he's in sick bay. Says it's rather urgent.'

Lynne glanced at the clock. Well, the department did owe her another five minutes. 'Thanks a lot.'

She walked rather soberly towards sick bay. Her feelings were a mixture of curiosity and annoyance. Trust Ben to mess things up, but perhaps it wasn't really his fault. It could all be due to Sarah Wishart.

The sight of Ben with his leg propped up on a fracture board and the bruises showing above the plaster back splint made her abandon the scolding she had rehearsed.

'Ben, how on earth—' she began.

Ben Gresham grinned ruefully. 'Trust to your Uncle Ben to make a muck of things! Remember last night when you broke my heart by turning down my invitation to dinner?'

Lynne nodded. 'I suppose you went and drowned your sorrows, or something silly!'

Ben jerked his head violently and then winced. 'I did nothing of the sort! I was walking back when I slipped—must have been a touch of frost on dead leaves or something. Down I went, all ten feet of me, and I must have caught my ankle on the curb. Did I feel a proper nitwit! There I was, almost within shouting distance of that famous hospital, St David's, a broken ankle and not a soul in sight—not even a light in the nearest houses. I was just making up my mind to try crawling when this little white car draws up. I think it was going to turn round, but luckily the driver didn't pass me off as a drunk, so—'

'So it was Dr Wishart, and she patched you up and drove you to Casualty and here you are,' Lynne interrupted briskly. 'I'm glad you're all right, but if I don't get back Dr Layton will be tearing his hair.'

'And that's more important than my restless and aching heart?' he demanded.

Lynne stared at him. 'Don't be silly! You're being properly looked after, aren't you?' She turned to go, then stopped. 'What I can't understand is why Sister Casualty should say Dr Wishart blamed herself for your accident?'

Ben chuckled. 'Well, if she hadn't blinded me with her headlights I would have seen the dead leaves or the frost, and you'd be working with me this afternoon instead of old Layton.'

'Timothy Layton isn't all that old,' Lynne said softly, and walked towards the door. 'Perhaps Dr Wishart will come and hold your hand later,' she added wickedly.

She heard Ben say something about their being all wrong about Sarah Wishart, but she didn't stop to contradict him. She wasn't sure whether to be annoyed or sick at heart at the way circumstances were changing.

There was no sign of Sister Casualty when Lynne got back. The junior nurse had one small boy sitting on the plaster table and the pair of them were chatting cheerfully.

'Where's Dr Layton?'

'There was a message to say he'd be a few minutes late. He had to see someone, Staff Nurse.'

Lynne turned towards her plaster trolley. She couldn't help wondering whether Sarah Wishart was making the most of her opportunities in that direction as well.

Timothy Layton came in on the tail of her thoughts, but he looked so pale and strained that she concentrated on getting the afternoon list of casualties finished as soon as possible. If they had been at Aunt Jenny's she could have told him frankly that he was overdoing it his first day back at work, but here at St David's she had to accept the constraint of being on duty. She could be informal with Ben Gresham when they were alone, but Timothy Layton was Senior Casualty Officer. Even now that their relations were more friendly than they had been before that awful tunnel incident she still couldn't speak out of turn.

Their last case was on the table and Lynne had sent the junior to tea when Timothy Layton put down the plaster bandage he was holding.

'Just finish it off, Staff Nurse, for me.' He got to his feet and swayed a little, but before Lynne could make a move, he had stumbled towards the door. His set stern face warned her against offering a helping hand.

'Doctor looks kind of done in, Nurse. Had a busy day, eh?'

Lynne rinsed the plaster off her hands. 'You can say that again, Mrs Wells! I've lost count. Dr Layton's been off ill and—'

'I remember now!' the woman broke in excitedly. 'Weren't you with him in that tunnel disaster?'

Lynne flushed a little and turned away to dry her hands. 'Our team was there,' she said stiffly.

She was thankful when the ambulance man appeared in the doorway. 'This the last patient, then, Staff Nurse?'

'Yes, John, Mrs Wells is truly the last one—I hope.'

The driver laughed. 'For a bit—it's thawing, you'll be pleased to hear, and rain's forecast for the next twenty-four hours. Come on, missus, let's be having you. Lean on me and hop—take your time.'

Methodically Lynne started to clear away the débris of the past few hours. She really should go and see if they were finished in Casualty Theatre. She knew she would have to encounter Sarah Wishart sooner or later. It was the thought of the mockery she was sure would be in the other woman's eyes that made her reluctant. Women like Sarah Wishart always seemed to have all the weapons and she wished she didn't feel so utterly defenceless. Ben's final remark had disturbed her more than she wanted to admit.

With a little sigh Lynne straightened her cap and left the plaster room to the final ministrations of her junior. She had almost reached Sister Casualty's office before she realised that the red-headed figure in the white coat talking to her senior must be Dr Wishart. Lynne stopped abruptly, sorely tempted to duck out of sight, when the other woman caught sight of her. She said something quickly to Sister Casualty and walked away, her light laughter ringing unpleasantly in Lynne's ears.

'Ah, there you are, Staff Nurse. I was just coming to look for you. Time you were off duty. There isn't anything the juniors can't manage. Junior Staff should be back from tea. Dr Layton gone?'

Lynne nodded, but before she could say anything, the other woman went on:

'I think it was a mistake his coming back so soon. Dr Wishart agrees with me. She says she will do the Casualty calls tonight and for the rest of the week.'

Lynne stifled a groan. Was there no limit to Sarah Wishart's influence? She had never expected that someone as hard-headed as Sister Casualty would be won over so easily.

'It was too bad that it had to be such a heavy list his first day on, Sister. John says the cold weather is over for the next twenty-four hours—' She tried to sound more light-hearted than she felt.

Sister Casualty snorted. 'Driver John and his weather forecasts! He always makes them at the end of his shift, knowing full well that if he's wrong it will be someone else's pigeon. Off you go, and thanks for all your hard work. I'm glad you and Dr Layton are no longer at odds.'

Lynne flushed, and the older woman chuckled. 'I suppose you thought I hadn't noticed! You forget I have trained eyes—I must say Junior Staff has pulled her weight today. Dr Wishart must have the right touch with that young lady.'

All the elation of the moment before drained out of Lynne. She felt utterly weary. 'Goodnight, Sister.' She turned away abruptly, afraid that her colleague would ask her what was wrong.

It wasn't until she had reached her room that Lynne remembered her promise to Timothy Layton. What a fool she had been to give it! All she wanted to do was to get out of her uniform, have a long soak in a lovely hot bath and potter around. The thought of having to get changed and to go out on a nasty rainy night to visit her godmother, who would probably slam the door in her face, appalled her. Maybe she should phone Aunt Jenny first, hoping that her offer of a visit would be turned down flat. Blast Timothy Layton, he had no business getting her involved in all this! It was all Sarah Wishart's fault. She couldn't even go and see Ben first. That wretched woman might be visiting him. Ben was bound to talk about her—

Aunt Jenny's face softened when she saw Lynne standing there on the doorstep. 'Come in, dear, you must be soaked. How sweet of you to come out on an evening like this. I was just about to make myself an omelette and have it in front of the fire. Like one, too, or have you eaten?'

'I'd love an omelette,' Lynne said gratefully. Her godmother had made it so easy for her—nothing to suggest that the scene of the other night had ever taken place.

It wasn't until they had finished their second cup of tea that Jenny Leslie mentioned her late guest. 'How did Timothy get on with his first day back?'

Lynne placed her empty cup back on the tray. 'I'm afraid it was a pretty heavy day,' she said slowly.

Jenny sniffed. 'I told him it was far too soon, but he wouldn't listen. He said your friend Ben was trying to do far too much on his own. By the way, why aren't you out with Ben tonight, or is he calling for you later?'

'He did ask me out for dinner, but unfortunately Ben slipped and broke his ankle,' Lynne explained carefully.

'You mean Timothy is doing Casualty single-handed when he isn't even a fit man?' Jenny demanded angrily.

Lynne hastily hid a smile at her godmother's vehemence and then, too late, realised where her answer would eventually lead her. 'Oh, Dr—I mean the locum who's standing in for Ben is doing the night calls for this week.'

'A locum at the hospital! He needs his head seen to.'

'It's a woman—someone who used to live in the area,' Lynne covered up, unhappily aware that Jenny Leslie would find out the truth for herself only too soon.

Blessedly the telephone rang and the older woman excused herself. 'It's for you, Lynne. Are you on call, then?'

Lynne got up hastily. Timothy Layton was the only one who knew where she was.

'It's a girl's voice,' her godmother said drily.

Lynne was thankful for the dim light in the hall. 'Staff Nurse Howard speaking.'

A rather high-pitched and breathless voice answered: 'I'm so glad I found you, Staff Nurse. It's Dr Layton I'm calling for, and it's urgent. He's in sick bay—the last door on the right. You're not to knock, just go right in.'

The receiver at the other end was put down before Lynne could ask a single question or even reprove the speaker for not identifying herself. Poor Timothy, he had gone back to work too soon, and it was partly her fault. If she hadn't burst out in her defence of Ben none of this would have happened. She went back to the sitting room thankful that her godmother couldn't have overheard the message.

'I'm sorry, Aunt Jenny, but I'll have to go back—it's an emergency.'

'Can't this woman locum of yours manage without you?' The older woman sounded amused.

'Oh, it isn't her, it's one of our own Casualty staff,' Lynne said quickly. 'I don't think it will take long.'

'I'm quite all right on my own, you know, but please yourself. That omelette offer still holds.'

Lynne avoided her godmother's eyes and picked up her coat. 'See you later. Sorry about this.'

As she hurried back to the hospital Lynne's thoughts were a mixture of concern for Timothy Layton and annoyance at the complications she was landing herself in. Instinctively she went up the fire stairs to the sick bay. There was no point in advertising that Dr Timothy Layton had sent for her again in a highly irregular way. She wondered who the caller had been. The voice was vaguely familiar, but too breathless to recognise with any certainty.

Cautiously Lynne pushed open the fire door and looked along the corridor. She must remember that she had come the back way so that Timothy Layton would be behind that door immediately on her left. There was very little light apart from the dull red glow of the fire exit lamp, but at least there was no one about. The girl had said not to knock, so Lynne opened the door swiftly and stepped through, into unexpected darkness. Before she could collect herself the door clicked shut behind her with an ominous snick. For an awful second Lynne felt all her old fears of dark places crowding back. She pulled herself together hastily and began to feel for the light switch. After a few minutes of frantic search she realised that not only was there no light switch, but the place was full of laundry hampers, wheelchairs and other heavy equipment. Worst of all, there was no handle on the inside of the door. She was firmly locked in the sick bay storeroom—in the dark, with equipment that certainly wasn't likely to be needed before morning and no one— no one at all knew where she was. Poor Timothy Layton, he would be wondering desperately why she hadn't come, but in the circumstances he wouldn't organise a search party. Lynne sat down forlornly on one of the hampers and pulled her coat more tightly round her. She tried not to think of how long she might be there. If things got too bad she might have to hammer on the door. Would anyone hear her? Ben was in the sick bay, but along at the other end of the corridor. Unless anyone was really ill the sick bay night nurse usually gave out the evening drinks and then helped on one of the wards until it was time for her to go to her own supper between eleven and midnight. Lynne shivered and then sat very still. She was sure she heard someone giggling and whispering quite close. But she must have been mistaken; there wasn't even a footstep—nothing but the beating of her own heart and the cold darkness closing round her.

## CHAPTER EIGHT

LYNNE was never quite sure how long she had been sitting in that dark cold storeroom. Without any warning at all the light was switched on, dazzling her. The door made a clicking sound as if someone were trying to open it. Then she distinctly heard someone walking away down the corridor. Without waiting for conscious decision Lynne stumbled towards the handleless door, her fingers scrabbling at the sharp edge. To her hysterical relief the panel came towards her, grudgingly at first, and then there was space for her to squeeze through. It wasn't until she was safely in the corridor that Lynne felt the sickening reaction of near panic. She was running down the corridor towards the main entrance to sick bay, not to the safe anonymity of the dimly lit fire stairs. It wasn't until she heard Ben's laughter coming from a half-open doorway that she realised what she was doing. Praying that Ben's visitors wouldn't glance out into the corridor, she tiptoed back down the passage. As the heavy fire door swung closed behind her Lynne leaned against the wall, sick and trembling.

After a few minutes she took herself severely in hand. She was absolutely convinced now that Timothy Layton was not in Sick Bay and never had been. It had to be someone who resented her friendship—off and on as it was—with Ben. It certainly was most unlikely that Dr Sarah Wishart would descend to such a prank. It could only be Bibs or some junior she had bullied into making

that hoax phone call. Lynne went cautiously down the
fire stairs and across the dark garden to the Nurses'
Home thankful that things had been no worse. No doubt
the hoaxers had expected to catch her outside Ben's
door. Bless him for laughing at the right moment and so
warning her. There was nothing more she could do
tonight.

Lynne went on duty a trifle apprehensively. One
glance at the work rota showed her that Dr Timothy
Layton was taking his normal sessions and that she
would be working with him. As she turned away from
the notice board she heard laughing coming from the
plaster room. It could only be Bibs. Lynne with a feeling
of unusual anger marched towards the door. To her
astonishment it was two of the juniors.

They blushed a little shyly when they saw her.

'Have you heard the latest about dear Bibs? Night
Sister ordered her out of Sick Bay—said she was being
too noisy!' Belatedly they remembered their manners.
'Sorry, Staff Nurse, we didn't mean to be cheeky.'

Lynne didn't have the heart to scold them. They could
have been so easily laughing about *her*. 'Don't let Sister
Casualty hear you. Have you got plenty of plaster
bandages?'

'Yes, Staff Nurse,' they chorused. 'We got them first
thing from the stores porter.'

Lynne continued on her way to Sister Casualty's
office. Last night's experience had shaken her. It was
something that could have happened to a junior, but
certainly not to a Sister Casualty-elect. The sooner she
learned how to control her impulsiveness the better.

Sister Casualty gave her senior staff nurse a tight little
smile. 'I hope we have a quiet day for a change. Another
session like yesterday and I'll need my retirement earlier
than planned!' Her tone was grim, and Lynne was

dismayed to see how weary the older woman was.

'Couldn't you have a holiday earlier than usual, Sister?' The words were out before Lynne realised they might have seemed tactless.

'And miss my annual journey through the bulb-fields? Or are you so anxious to take over, Staff Nurse?' but there was a gentle teasing note now in Sister Casualty's voice. Then more briskly: 'Time we started work—that sounds like the first load of casualties.'

Lynne was thankful that the first two hours of the morning were too busy for her to steal more than a quick look at Timothy Layton. Granted he still looked tired, but his face had lost that drawn pallor of yesterday. With a faint feeling of panic Lynne wondered what he would have said if he had known about that faked message.

A junior brought them cups of coffee just after eleven. 'Sister Casualty asked me to let you know that there's been another pile-up on the motorway, sir.'

Timothy Layton groaned. 'These freezing fogs—what a pity they ever invented fast cars! Thanks, Nurse. Pity you couldn't have brought some instant energy as well.'

He turned to Lynne after the girl had gone. 'Did you see Jenny last night?'

Lynne nodded, hesitating as to whether she should tell him why she had been called away. The noise of approaching stretchers saved her from answering.

It was two o'clock when they finally cleared the decks. For the past half hour Sister Casualty had been hovering like a mother bird.

'Off you go, Staff Nurse. I've told the dining room to save your meal. Dr Layton, I've told the Central Bureau that we can't take any more emergencies unless there's a national disaster until after five. Dr Wishart has two more cases in Casualty Theatre, so I suggest you take a break until three o'clock. I promise not to call you before then. I've told Matron I couldn't let any nurses off duty this morning.'

Timothy Layton winked at Lynne as they washed the plaster off their hands. 'You have to hand it to the old dear—she really looks after us. I suppose I should have offered to relieve Sarah, but at least she's younger than I am. I don't see things easing up unless we have a blizzard or a flood to tie the cars down. Mad fools, I think some of them must have a death wish—like those silly lemmings. Are you on this afternoon?'

Lynne shook her head. 'Not until five o'clock.'

'Meet me for coffee in half an hour,' he said quickly. 'I'd say lunch, but Sister Casualty has arranged that for you. Be at the coffee bar on the corner.'

Lynne nodded, conscious that one of the juniors was coming their way.

Timothy Layton let Lynne go first. She had reached the dining room corridor when she saw Bibs coming towards her. Lynne pretended to be too absorbed in a letter she had collected from Reception to notice her junior colleague. She wished she had the courage to confront the girl and accuse her of last night's outrage, but supposition was one thing and accusation was another. The encounter with Bibs had taken away the last shreds of her appetite and she was glad to escape. If she hurried she could change out of uniform. The coffee bar wasn't out of bounds, but somehow she felt she would be too conspicuous sitting with Timothy Layton.

The Senior Casualty Officer was waiting for her. 'I ordered for you—coffee and apple tart.' He smiled at her surprise. 'Warmed-up meals aren't much when you've gone past your mealtime. Listen, Lynne, I feel I owe you some explanation.'

She stared at him. Surely he wasn't going to talk about

Sarah Wishart *here*? He saw her expression and put his hand momentarily over hers.

'Perhaps you're right, Lynne. It's all old history now. Once Ben is back we can return to normal. I feel that we've been living from one crisis to another ever since that wretched tunnel disaster. I wish I didn't have that school lecture to give tomorrow. We could have driven out into the country somewhere.'

Lynne was puzzled. It was almost as if he were talking to someone else. Had his weariness clouded his memory and did he think she was Sarah Wishart again?

The coffee and apple pie arrived and Lynne busied herself with the welcome snack. It had been a mistake to get involved with Timothy Layton in the first place, but of course none of it had been her intention. Events had hustled them into a relationship—if one could call it that—and now she seemed to occupy a place in his confidence that she didn't deserve and didn't want. Part of her had been flattered by the attentions of an older man. It would be a pity if he had read something in to their friendship that didn't exist. Suddenly she realised that he was talking again.

'I didn't realise how much I needed the companionship of someone like you, my dear. You never make demands and you always seem to understand. You're so—peaceful.'

Hastily Lynne drained her coffee cup. 'I'd better be going, Timothy.'

He looked startled. 'But I thought you were off until five. I brought my car. Wouldn't you like a drive, since I can't take you tomorrow?'

Lynne hesitated and was lost. Timothy took her by the arm, throwing some coins on the counter as they passed. It wasn't until they were in the car and heading for the country that Lynne found her voice again.

'Sister Casualty was talking about her retirement this morning,' she said brightly.

Timothy Layton gave her a curious glance. 'Is she? I suppose she's getting on. I wonder who'll take her place? One of those dedicated career types, I suppose—not that we can do without them. It seems such a waste.'

Lynne swallowed hastily. 'I'm supposed to take over after Easter,' she said in a very small voice.

The car took a leap forward and it was several moments before Timothy had it under smooth control again. 'You! I don't believe it! You've got blood in your veins, not embalming fluid!'

Lynne was hurt. 'Sister Casualty has been training me for the takeover for the past six months,' she said stiffly.

'I don't care if she's been training you for six years, it's ridiculous! I shall tell her so,' Timothy said with unexpected vehemence. 'What does your godmother think—if she knows?'

'The same as you—she wants me to go abroad with her,' Lynne admitted reluctantly. Somehow they seemed to have slipped back to square one, to the days when Dr Layton thought she could do nothing right.

'That would be even worse!' Timothy retorted. 'That's existing, not living. No, you should marry and bring up a family, like your parents before you.'

Lynne held her breath. If this was intended as a proposal it was the most indirect one she had ever heard. Then recklessly she plunged in:

'And who do you think I should marry?'

'Whom—' he corrected absently. 'Why, young Ben Gresham would do nicely for a start.'

'It sounds as if you expect me to marry several times,' Lynne flashed. 'Anyway, he's got his future to establish. It will be years yet.'

Timothy Layton swung the car off the main road into a

convenient lay-by. 'Well, my dear, you know best which direction your heart may lead you. If I were younger, and there was no one else you wanted, I might even ask you myself.'

Lynne felt her cheeks stinging. How completely she had misread him—all he wanted to do was to play uncle! 'Thanks—thanks a lot. I'm twenty-three, not sweet seventeen, you know.'

He chuckled. 'I like you when you're angry, Lynne. You're human then, and not dedicated and—desiccated like Sister Casualty.'

'She's been very good to me,' Lynne defended her colleague.

'Has she? She's been feeding on your youth and strength like a parasite. That's the trouble with hospitals. Better if they had remained as annexes to nunneries and monasteries. That way a lot of youthful energy and enthusiasm would have been better applied.'

'You mean we should have been out demonstrating with the rest?' Lynne demanded. 'For that matter, how come *you* stayed with the hospital service?' She knew she was being rude, but he had started it.

He sighed. 'I suppose I used it like a monk his monastery—to get away from a human situation that I couldn't deal with.'

'You mean Sarah?' Lynne ventured.

He nodded. 'Odd how we always keep coming back to her. I thought I'd put it all behind me. I can't help wondering why she's come back. Let's talk about something else, Lynne. I can't take even your gentle probing today. I know a place where we can sit by the fire, have a home-made tea. I'll get you back by five.'

Lynne hesitated. 'But I thought you were taking over at three.'

'I know that's what your boss said, but I'm not. I'm

taking the night calls instead, by mutual arrangement.'

Something in his expression warned Lynne not to trespass further. For the rest of the afternoon they talked about general things. She enjoyed their tea in front of a blazing log fire and was surprised to learn that Timothy enjoyed books and music as much as she did.

'Not the modern stuff,' he admitted. 'Or the permissive society—you can have them or chuck them in the ocean for all I care.'

'But you're a rebel,' Lynne ventured.

'Was,' he corrected. 'It's mostly bad temper now and lack of patience. I know what I like and I don't really care whether the other chap does or not. That Ben Gresham of yours, he's got strong ideas, too, but of course he covers it up with all that tomfoolery.'

'He's not mine,' Lynne objected.

'I meant your generation, not your personal property,' Timothy rebuked her gently. 'I'd be happier if you were more of a rebel.'

Lynne stared at him in astonishment. 'But why? It's not the way to get on—not in nursing, anyway.'

Timothy made an impatient gesture. 'You've been brainwashed, that's why. I suppose we'd better be starting back. Thank you for coming with me. I've enjoyed this afternoon.'

With a sudden flash of insight Lynne realised that Timothy Layton was a very lonely man. Perhaps that was why they got on.

As if he had read her thought, 'It takes loneliness to understand loneliness, but you shouldn't be at your age. I suppose you're an only child and your parents are miles away—in spirit, I mean.'

Lynne felt uneasy. This man was seeing too much. 'Something like that,' she had admitted. 'Now I hate to hurry you, but I have to change before I go on duty.'

'Sorry, I forgot.'

Lynne was glad to find that everything was quiet in the department when she got back. Sister Casualty had gone to tea. Bibs had been sent off early—the junior didn't know why.

'I think Sister Casualty was telling her off, but that's just guessing. Dear Bibs was very pink about the gills when she came out of the office. What do you want me to do now, Staff Nurse?'

Lynne surveyed the scene. It looked so peaceful after this morning. 'Make up stock, I think. You never know what's going to turn up.'

'Oh, there was a message for you, Staff Nurse. One of the porters brought it over. I put it in your locker—the note, I mean.'

Lynne hid her surprise. It all sounded cloak and dagger. For a moment she wondered if it were a follow-up of last night's hoax. She shivered a little as she remembered her ordeal in the dark storeroom.

Lynne glanced curiously at the envelope as she took it from the top shelf of her locker. Opening the note, she saw it was from Ben.

'Have I offended you, Lynne? If so, I'm sorry. Your Uncle Ben is feeling very full of self-pity. I sent a message last night. I suppose you were out. Hope to see you later,

Uncle Ben.'

Lynne stared down at the piece of paper rather grimly. So there had been a message last night—a genuine one. Had someone altered the name for some reason of their own? Well, puzzling over it wouldn't solve it. Perhaps Ben could throw some light on the hoax, if she decided to tell him. They had shared so many things in the past.

Was she going to allow Dr Sarah Wishart to spoil this friendship too?

It was eight-thirty when Lynne left Casualty. A local accident had held her up at the last moment. However, the injuries were minor and she hadn't called Timothy Layton out. Perhaps she should have, but she felt oddly reluctant to meet him face to face quite yet.

Lynne hesitated before knocking on Ben's door, but there was no sound of voices or casual laughter.

Ben hitched himself up on his pillows as she came in and his face lighted up. 'I thought you weren't coming, Lynne. I'd given you up. Late case?'

Lynne sat down wearily. 'The terrible twins again. I think they hunt accidents!'

Ben chuckled. 'I'm sure of it. Whenever they get bored they go in search of broken glass, rusty nails—the lot. I thought you might have come this afternoon, but I gather you went out for a drive instead.'

Lynne flushed. She could never get used to the efficiency of the hospital grapevine. 'I needed some fresh air,' she said curtly. 'Anyway, I wasn't so sure you wanted more visitors. You sounded happy enough last—' she stopped abruptly. She hadn't intended to say anything as yet.

'Last night? You mean you came over but didn't come in? There was only Bibs and Grant here, and they were too busy giggling about something to be much company.'

Lynne gritted her teeth. She had never suspected Peter Grant, but perhaps he had thought it amusing. No doubt Bibs had put him up to it—or at least counted him in. Had he been the one to turn on the light? The footsteps had sounded heavier than a nurse's.

'What's eating you, Lynne? You look furious enough to start on me.'

Lynne decided she might as well tell him. 'Someone locked me in the sick bay storeroom last night.'

'You mean when you were on your way to see me?'

Lynne had forgotten that there was more than one half to the story. 'I had a message to say that old Timothy had collapsed and was asking for me.' She braced herself for Ben's derision.

'So that's what happened,' Ben said thoughtfully. 'Bibs swore she had sent my message, but she didn't say she'd twisted it. No wonder they were snickering. And you fell for it?'

Lynne nodded. 'It sounded so urgent and he had looked ghastly when we finished yesterday—even Sister Casualty commented on it.'

Ben looked at her flushed face keenly. 'You falling for old Timothy or something?'

'Would you care if I was?' Lynne demanded hotly.

Ben chuckled. 'Keep your shirt on, old girl. I need notice of such a question. A chap like me with his way to make can't go committing himself.'

Lynne was about to dispute this when there was a brisk tap on the door and Dr Sarah Wishart came in. She didn't see Lynne at first.

'Sorry I didn't get over earlier, Ben, but I got called away—some urgent business. I brought you some beer. Got any glasses?' It was then that Lynne stood up. 'Oh, sorry, I didn't see you there, Staff Nurse. I expect you're on your way off duty.'

Lynne found herself outside the door seething with anger. That wretched woman had the knack of dismissing her as if she were a mere junior. She could hear Ben calling her, but she didn't go back. She was wasting her time here anyway. Timothy had been all wrong when he had suggested that she and Ben were two of a kind. She thought wistfully of this afternoon—it had all been so pleasant, with no interruptions. At least, not of the physical kind—she had to admit that Sarah Wishart had come into the conversation.

Lynne was almost ready for bed when she remembered her godmother. It was too late to keep her promise to Timothy Layton tonight, but she could phone. Shivering a little, she went along to the kiosk in the front hall. She could hear the ringing at the other end, but there was no reply. Perhaps Jenny Leslie had gone out—or was having an early night. Feeling guilty, Lynne went off to bed. She had tried and that was that. Today had been full of 'tries' that hadn't quite come off. Rather grimly she resolved not to get so involved with people tomorrow.

She must have fallen into a very heavy sleep. Someone was shaking her very vigorously. 'Staff Nurse, you're wanted in Casualty. It's urgent. Dr Layton said to tell you it's a major crash.'

Lynne sat up abruptly. 'Oh, no, you don't get me that way.' It took the girl's startled face to make Lynne realise that this message was genuine. 'Sorry, I was half asleep. I'll be right over.'

Casualty seemed to be full of moaning and crying people. Night Sister and two juniors were trying to sort out the chaos. The older woman caught sight of Lynne and came over. 'Thank goodness you weren't out, Staff Nurse. Sorry to drag you over. If you'll help Dr Layton in Casualty Theatre I think Dr Grant can manage the fractures. It would happen tonight when the wards are so busy. I don't want to call Sister Casualty if it can be helped.

'We'll manage,' Lynne reassured her, and with a little thrill of excitement she went to help Timothy.

If he was pleased to see her, he gave no sign, only a curt little nod. 'Get me some gossamer silk, Staff Nurse.

Your junior doesn't seem to know what I want.'

Smoothly Lynne took over from the frightened junior and sent her to prepare the next case. She had to admire the way Timothy coped with the situation. Refusing to be hurried, he worked his way through the list of casualties that Lynne and the junior presented and yet found time to reassure his patients with a quiet word or a simple joke.

It was midnight when they straightened their aching shoulders as the last patient was eased off the theatre table.

'Good girl,' Timothy said simply. Lynne untied his gown and turned to tackle the mess.

'Leave it, Staff Nurse,' Night Sister said crisply from the doorway. 'There's tea and sandwiches in Sister Casualty's office. I've been on to the Central Bureau— they've struck us off the emergency list for the next twelve hours.'

'Seems to me I heard that earlier on today—or was it yesterday? Thanks, Night Sister. Luckily none of these cases required admission. What about Dr Grant's?'

'One fractured pelvis admitted, the rest sent home in plaster to come back for check-up X-rays.'

So once again Lynne found herself having tea with Timothy Layton, but this time both of them were too tired for conversation other than the occasional disjointed phrase.

'I chose the right night to take over for Sarah Wishart!' Timothy said finally, and stood up to go.

Lynne wondered what he would say if she told him what Sarah Wishart had done with at least part of her evening, but Timothy was gone with a brief goodnight before she could summon the energy.

Night Sister stopped Lynne as she was leaving. 'Sister Casualty says you're not to come on until lunchtime.'

This time Lynne was past surprise—hospital grape-vines even reached senior colleagues in their sleep!

It was eleven a.m. before Lynne finally climbed back to reality. It took her several minutes before she remembered what had happened. As she swung her feet on to the floor she saw that someone had pushed a note under the door. Picking it up sleepily, she stared at it for a moment uncomprehendingly. The name Mrs Jenkins didn't register at first until she saw her godmother's phone number underneath. Someone had scribbled 'urgent—phoned twice' in the bottom corner.

With a feeling of shocked surprise Lynne hastily dressed and went down to the front hall to phone.

Mrs Jenkins' voice sounded very troubled at the other end of the line. 'I don't knows what to think, Nurse. Mrs Leslie said nothing last night about going away sudden like. How do I know? Simple—the bed's not been slept in and her big cases are gone from the top of the wardrobe, and her car ain't in the garridge. I know, 'cos I looked.'

Lynne tried to make some sense out of all this. 'When did you see Mrs Leslie last?'

'Oh, I sees what you mean. It was about nine-thirty. She had friends in for supper and I stayed on to do the clearing up. They'd just gone before I was getting my hat and coat on. Something had been said about a dance earlier on. I think, but I can't be sure, that Mrs Leslie was to follow on. Then just as I was going out the back I heard the front doorbell. I thought maybe one of the others had come back to hurry her up, but I didn't stop. Weren't none of my business.'

Lynne had listened carefully. 'Did you see anyone as you came away—a car or anything at all, Mrs Jenkins?'

'Let me see, it was kind of dark and I was in a hurry to get home. Ron doesn't like it when I stop out too late, even though we needs the money with him still off heavy work. Oh, yes, I saw a white car—a Mini, maybe. Seems I've seen it about before, but it could have been a different one.'

Lynne tried not to let her imagination gallop away with her. The late caller didn't *have* to be Dr Sarah Wishart. 'Did Mrs Leslie leave you a note, Mrs Jenkins?'

'Nothing that I could see lying about, Nurse. It wasn't as if she hadn't told me what she wanted done today. It's only that if she's been called away sudden like, I was counting on the money.'

Lynne thought rapidly. She had a few pounds in her purse. 'How much does my godmother owe you, Mrs Jenkins?'

The woman sounded very apologetic. 'I hates to bother you, Nurse, but you know how it is. Ten pounds, near enough, though I could manage with less.'

'Can you hang on for ten minutes, Mrs Jenkins? I'll be right over.'

'Thanks ever so, Nurse. I'll make some coffee for you. Mrs Leslie would expect me to.'

Lynne didn't argue. She felt suddenly very empty. Tea and sandwiches in the middle of the night didn't make up for going without breakfast.

A quick survey of her godmother's home made it perfectly clear that the older woman had departed and apparently intended to stay away more than a few days. There was absolutely nothing anyone could do until Jenny Leslie got in touch. Lynne wondered if she should phone home. Perhaps her mother would have heard from her.

Mrs Jenkins came into the sitting room to collect the coffee tray. 'Proper mystery it is, Nurse. I don't know rightly what to do. Usually I comes in three times a week—and extra if Mrs Leslie is having a party or a din-

ner. She's given me a key. Should I hand it in to you,
like?'

Lynne sighed. 'I'm sure she'll be in touch. You'd
better come in as usual, even if just to check that
everything's all right. You'd better stop the milk and
bread—just tell them that Mrs Leslie will let them know
when to start delivering again. I expect she'll let the post
office know about letters. By the way, were there any
this morning?'

Mrs Jenkins stared at her. 'Never thought of looking
in the box—never been part of what you might call my
duties.'

Lynne stood up. 'I'll have a look, just in case.'

There *was* an envelope in Jenny Leslie's handwriting
addressed to Mrs Jenkins.

The cleaning woman was most apologetic. 'If I'd only
thought of looking I needn't have bothered you.' She
took out a sheet of notepaper and two five-pound notes.
'You'd better read it, Nurse, and then you'll know for
sure what's happened.'

There were only a few lines, mostly along the lines
Lynne had already suggested and saying that the writer
would be in touch. She handed it back.

'It looks as if we've been worrying ourselves for
nothing. I expect one of her friends asked her for a
week's visit on the spur of the moment. I'd better be
getting back. Thanks for the coffee. All right now, Mrs
Jenkins?'

The woman nodded. 'I reckon it has to be. I still thinks
it odd her going off so sudden and taking the big cases.'

'Could be a house party with a lot going on,' Lynne
suggested with a reassuring smile. 'You know where to
get in touch with me if you're worried about anything,
Mrs Jenkins.'

Lynne walked rapidly back to the Nurses' Home. She

wished she felt as sure as she had sounded. Sudden journeys weren't in character. There must have been something to upset her, but at least she had remembered about Mrs Jenkins' wages. So it couldn't have been a decision taken in blind panic. It was silly to connect every white car with the red-headed newcomer in Casualty.

But the telegram waiting for Lynne brought uneasiness back. It had been handed in at Dover:

'Off to Paris and parts unknown—don't know when I'll be back. No address for now, and don't tell anyone where I am unless absolutely necessary. Love, Jay.' It had to be from Jenny Leslie and there was nothing Lynne could do but wait. She couldn't even tell Timothy of the latest development or Ben or anyone at all. No doubt Mrs Jenkins would be looked after with separate instructions.

Lynne changed into uniform and went off to first lunch feeling very puzzled indeed. She was halfway through her meal when she saw Bibs come in. To her astonishment her junior colleague came stalking over.

'Trust you to get extra time off when I've got a special date tonight. I suppose you got your precious Timothy Layton to wangle things for you!'

The discourtesy was bad enough, but the unfairness was worse. 'Night Sister told me to, and it had nothing to do with Dr Layton. If you like, I'll do second call tonight. I'm not going out.'

Bibs didn't even have the decency to be gracious. 'I suppose you know that Dr Layton has a lecture tonight—at least Dr Wishart won't spoil your ladyship.'

This time Lynne struck back. 'I don't have to do second call for you,' she reminded her junior.

This time her colleague flushed a little. 'Well, thanks—see you later.'

Lynne went on duty unhappily. No matter what she did or how hard she tried there was always someone who objected. She had done her best to get on with Bibs, but the girl was becoming impossible. Whether it was envy or jealousy or just downright incompatibility she didn't know. She could only pray that Matron would give her someone else as senior staff nurse when she took over from Sister Casualty. Otherwise life was going to be one lengthy tug-of-war.

Sister Casualty greeted Lynne warmly. 'I almost wished I hadn't told you to take the morning off. There's been a go-slow in all departments this morning. Dr Layton and Dr Wishart aren't speaking. Someone made two of the juniors cry. And they forgot to cross St David's off the major take-in. It's been bedlam.' She smiled a little at Lynne's concerned face. 'It's all right, the worst of the rush is over. We're only on for minor casualties this afternoon—that should help—and the bottleneck in X-Ray should have cleared itself by now. They were short-handed because of your little do in the night. Be a little tactful with Junior Staff—she's got a hate on because she has to do second call tonight. I'll be off now.'

Sister Casualty was out of sight by the time Lynne remembered that she was doing Bibs' second call. It couldn't be helped and it shouldn't make much difference. It was the older woman's half day, and the change in the duty rota might just not reach her via the hospital grapevine.

Lynne checked the duty sheet and the stores book before she went around the department. The juniors on this afternoon had finished clearing up and were busy replenishing stock or doing their weekly chores. For a change the benches in Casualty were empty and there was no sign of either Casualty Officer. Perhaps both Dr

Timothy Layton and Dr Sarah Wishart were at lunch, or they could have gone to the Clinical Meeting. Switchboard would know where to find them if anything turned up that she couldn't cope with.

The juniors seemed pleased to see her. 'Thank goodness you're back, Staff Nurse! We almost handed in our resignations this morning.'

Lynne looked properly sympathetic. 'What upset you this time?'

'Dear Bibs put the blame on us for not checking the splints cupboard when she knew perfectly well it was her job. That Dr Wishart was narked with us as well. I suppose she was up in the night too.'

Lynne knew perfectly well that they were using her as a safety valve. 'Only Dr Layton was in Casualty last night,' she pointed out reasonably.

'Well, she must have been out on the razzle, then. She was all heavy-eyed and bad-tempered into the bargain. We couldn't do anything right.'

Lynne heard the footsteps. 'It's probably Junior Staff,' she warned.

'Oh, she'll be in X-Ray for ages yet. There are three casualties down there still. Sister told her to relieve Nurse Miller as soon as she came back from lunch. Two of the technicians didn't come in today because they were called out in the night.'

Lynne held up an admonitory finger and they took the hint. She went to see who their visitor was.

Dr Sarah Wishart was standing in the corridor outside Sister Casualty's office. She frowned when she saw Lynne. 'Where's everyone? Haven't you got anything better to do than gossip, Staff Nurse?'

Lynne's shoulders stiffened. 'We're only on for minor casualties this afternoon, Dr Wishart. Is there something coming in, then?'

The other woman moved irritably. 'That's your job, not mine. I suppose Sister is off duty?'

'It's her half day, Dr Wishart. Can I do something for you?' Lynne wished the locum Junior Casualty Officer would go away and leave her in peace.

'There is not! Is Dr Layton in the department?' It was obvious that even to put the question was distasteful.

Lynne shook her head with a proper show of regret. 'I'm afraid not, Dr Wishart. I expect he's at the Clinical Meeting.'

'Clinical Meeting? No one told me there was one.'

Lynne was only human. 'Perhaps they didn't think you'd be interested since you're temporary, Dr Wishart,' she suggested politely.

The older woman flushed. 'There's no need to be insolent, Staff Nurse! Since when have medical staff appointments been in your province, I'd like to know!' She turned on her heel and stalked out of the department.

For a moment Lynne had a feeling of elation, but it soon faded. The juniors had been right. Sarah Wishart looked as if she indeed had been up most of the night. Perhaps she had had something to do with Jenny Leslie's sudden departure. Lynne sighed. It was all very disturbing. She would be very glad when Ben was well enough to come back on duty.

Lynne heard someone coming. Oh dear, was Sarah Wishart coming back? However, this time it was Timothy Layton. Lynne greeted him warily.

'No cases in at the moment, Dr Layton. I'm keeping my fingers crossed.'

'Good,' he said absently. 'I'm trying to prepare my lecture for this evening. I went to the Clinical Meeting, but there wasn't anything in my line. That's the drawback to Casualty work—it isn't exactly medical progress or research. Has anyone—been looking for me?' He looked almost as reluctant as Sarah Wishart had been to put the question.

'The Junior Casualty Officer was here a few minutes ago,' Lynne said drily.

Timothy Layton flushed. 'I know I shouldn't ask, but is she still in a bad mood?'

Lynne had to smile. 'She certainly wasn't all cheery smiles. I don't think she likes me.'

'I don't think she likes women—or even men at times. By the way, I forgot to ask you if you'd been over to your godmother's last night?'

'She had a dinner party last night and I think they were going on to a dance later. There wasn't a reply when I rang.' Too late Lynne realised she had volunteered too much information in her attempts to conceal her god-mother's sudden departure.

Timothy looked at her keenly. 'Something's hap-pened, hasn't it?'

Lynne felt thoroughly uncomfortable. 'She's gone abroad for a while.'

Timothy Layton pounced on her reluctant statement. 'You're sure Jenny's all right? How do you know, anyway?'

'Mrs Jenkins, the cleaning woman, phoned me this morning. I went over, but we found a note from Aunt Jenny.'

'And—?'

Blast the man, he was worse than a TV detective! 'I had a telegram from Dover saying she was going to France—to Paris first and then touring—and there'd be no address for the time being.' If she hadn't still been worried about her godmother Lynne wouldn't have told him anything at all. She wished she knew how good friends they had been.

'You're still not telling me everything, are you? Come on, Lynne, it could be important.'

'Very friendly with Staff Nurse, aren't you, Timothy?' came Sarah Wishart's sneering voice from just behind them. 'I thought you swore there was nothing—nothing at all—in the rumours!'

## CHAPTER NINE

BEFORE Lynne could explode into justified anger Timothy had taken command of the situation.

'Lynne's godmother went away unexpectedly, and naturally she's worried. So am I, for that matter. She was very good to me after my accident, don't forget.'

Sarah Wishart's face went scarlet and then white. 'I'm not likely to forget—ever! I know what that woman's so-called goodness means, as you never could!'

She walked away abruptly, leaving Lynne and Timothy staring after her.

The Casualty Officer had a stricken look. 'There's something going on that we don't know about. For God's sake, Lynne, if you do know anything, tell me.'

Reluctantly Lynne told him about the white Mini— about her fears that Sarah Wishart was threatening Jenny Leslie. She waited for Timothy to tell her that she was letting her imagination take wings.

But he didn't. 'Leave it with me, Lynne. I think part of this belongs to the past. It could account for a lot of things. See you in the morning.'

It was only when the Casualty Officer had gone that Lynne remembered that if she did get an accident case in she would be forced to call Dr Wishart. For a moment she had the wild idea that she would run out into the street and warn everyone not to get hurt until tomorrow. Then the sheer silliness of the notion struck her and she was almost reduced to giggling all on her own. Of course Timothy Layton would have gone to his lecture.

Lynne decided to take a gamble on Casualty's remain-

ing quiet and tackled the instrument cupboards on
Casualty Theatre. She sent one junior to tea and gave
the other the job of polishing the glass shelves and doors.
She didn't know what Bibs was doing, but the occasional
burst of laughter from the plaster room suggested that
the junior staff nurse wasn't spending all her time cleaning. Lynne wondered if Peter Grant had slipped away
from his ward duties for a brief interval of light
entertainment. She gave herself a little shake. She was in
danger of condemning everyone for enjoying a little
respite from the tension and tragedy of Casualty simply
because she wasn't having fun herself. She sighed. If
only Ben was back on duty—it seemed months since he
had damaged his ankle. With a feeling of shock she
realised that this was the second time today that she had
missed Ben. Perhaps it was a little trail of angry frustra-
tion that had lingered after Sarah Wishart had so high-
handedly interrupted her visit to Ben in sick bay.

The junior came back from tea. 'I hear Dr Gresham's
been discharged from Sick Bay, Staff Nurse. It's more
fun when he's around.'

Lynne had to restrain herself from agreeing with the
other's unspoken condemnation of Dr Wishart. She was
about to send the other junior to tea when the door of
the plaster room opened and she could clearly hear Ben
Gresham's voice:

'You watch it, Bibs—one of these days someone will
do you a mischief!'

Lynne didn't wait. She turned to the startled junior.
'Come on, Nurse Matson, we'll both go to tea now.
You'll know where we are if we're needed.'

She didn't notice that she was almost running until a
breathless Nurse Matson called out imploringly:

'Staff Nurse, wait for me!'

When Lynne got back to the department the plaster

room door was wide open and the room was both empty and tidy.

The other junior greeted her. 'Junior Staff has gone to tea—she had to collect something from the cleaner's. She said that there were no messages.'

Lynne longed to ask if Ben Gresham had left any word for her, but she didn't have the nerve to ask. Fortunately Nurse Matson wasn't so shy.

'Did Dr Gresham say when he was coming back to Casualty?'

The other girl shrugged. 'I don't suppose he got the chance. Dear Bibs and Dr Grant were so busy teasing him about the way he handled his crutches that he could not get a word in to them, let alone to me, if they even saw me.'

Lynne was too relieved to know that Ben hadn't been alone with Bibs to feel hurt that he hadn't enquired for her. No doubt finding Bibs on duty he had assumed that Lynne was off. Of course the other girl was quite capable of suppressing the fact that they were both in the department.

'Come on, girls, if we don't get those instruments finished you'll be late for supper.'

The threat to two perpetually-hungry juniors was enough to goad them into efficient action. Work progressed so well that Lynne felt magnanimous enough to tell Bibs that she could go to second supper and needn't bother to report back. Since Casualty was only on for minor accidents the department was very well covered without her disturbing presence. Lynne refused to admit that she was allowing personalities to creep into her behaviour. Surely for once she could allow herself to be human?

The phone rang as Lynne came back from supper. She expected that it would be a routine enquiry for one of the doctors. It took several seconds for the words at the other end to penetrate. Lynne had to ask the switchboard operator to repeat the message.

'It's Swithin Road School, Staff Nurse. There's been a terrible accident—children crushed. The ambulance will be bringing the cases here—it's closest. Dr Layton said it's a full-scale emergency.'

Lynne had summoned the juniors and started emergency procedure before the significance of the final part of the operator's message sank in. Swithin Road School—that must have been where Timothy Layton had gone to give his lecture. Dear God, his lecture had been on fire *prevention*—something must have gone terribly wrong. Nothing had been said about a fire.

The ringing of the ambulance sirens warned Lynne and her little team that their first casualties were about to arrive. She'd sent a message to the Common Room for Dr Wishart and asked switchboard to catch Bibs before she left the dining room. Matron would have been notified and no doubt would sent extra staff once the situation was assessed.

Once the ambulance men started bringing in the children Lynne knew that she was going to be stretched to the limit. So many of the first children were on oxygen that Casualty began to look like Cape Kennedy. Lynne felt sick when she saw the bruised faces, the pinched nostrils as the children struggled against the handicap of crushed ribs—so many had obviously been trampled on in a blind panic rush. X-Ray had sent up both its portable machines—the children would be in too fragile a condition for much handling.

Out of the corner of her eye Lynne saw Timothy Layton come in, walking alongside a stretcher holding a transfusion flask. She started to move towards him and stopped abruptly. This man whose face was a fixed frozen mask would never even notice her presence. She watched him walk past Sarah Wishart without even an acknowledgment. Whatever had happened back at Swithin Road School it was plain that Timothy Layton held himself responsible.

Lynne felt someone touch her on the shoulder and turned to see Sister Casualty's strained face.

'I've never seen anything like it, even in the blitz, but of course we were lucky in the war. They'd sent most of the children into the country from this area. Where's Junior Staff?'

Too late Lynne remembered that she had never told Sister Casualty about the change in the on call rota. 'It's my fault, Sister. I told her she could go. My being off this morning spoilt things for her date tonight.'

Sister Casualty nodded absently as if this were something that could be left until later. 'As long as you sent word for her recall, Staff Nurse. Can you give Dr Wishart a hand and I'll take Dr Layton's cases in Casualty Theatre.'

Lynne made no objection to the reversal of her usual role. This was no time for personal feelings. Dr Wishart acknowledged her with a curt nod. The plaster room had been turned into a second theatre with dressing trolleys laid up as quickly as the juniors could manage instead of the usual boxes of plaster bandages. Lynne had to admire the gentle but swift efficiency with which Sarah Wishart dealt with each child. The abrasions were cleansed and dressed, damaged ribs carefully strapped, legs and arms quickly but thoroughly checked, and splinted or put in plaster. There was little fuss or mess and it was all done so quietly that Lynne found herself working better than ever. There were even moments of mutual approval as she or Sarah Wishart moved to a similar action at the same time.

At last the steady stream of children began to slow down. Dr Wishart glanced across at Lynne.

'Could you do a quick check, Staff Nurse? We could do with a breather before long.'

Lynne saw the clock with disbelief as she came out into the main hall of Casualty. Nine o'clock—it simply couldn't be! She straightened her stiff shoulders and went in search of Casualty Sister. Lynne couldn't believe her eyes when she saw that the masked figure on the stool in Casualty Theatre was Ben. His crutches stood defiantly in a corner. There was no sign of the Senior Casualty Officer.

Casualty Sister beckoned Lynne over. 'We've got one more case and I think there are a couple of leg plasters for Dr Wishart.' She nodded in Ben's direction. 'Dr Layton was on the point of collapse and I had to order him out of the department. Dr Grant's taken him off to his quarters and if he's got any sense he'll give him a stiff sedative. I've never known a man take things so hard.'

Lynne risked a question. 'What happened—at the school, I mean?'

The older woman looked grim. 'I'm not completely sure, but I think someone let off a smoke bomb and all hell was let loose. I believe Dr Layton had taken some for demonstration purposes. I suppose some irresponsible youngster thought he'd have a bit of a lark— God forgive the little devil, whoever he was. I wouldn't want his conscience. Matron said she'd got hold of Junior Staff—the girl's supposed to be making tea for everyone. Perhaps you'd better check.'

Lynne found Bibs in the little kitchen attached to the Casualty canteen. Her face was pale and she'd obviously been crying. Trays of cups were lined up and she was dishing out milk and sugar.

'Are you ready yet, Staff Nurse? Isn't it terrible—

those poor kids! Why didn't you call me?'

Lynne hadn't the heart to be down on the girl. 'I tried, but I must have just missed you. So much was happening all at once—perhaps switchboard put other calls through first. There are about three children left to see to. You could give out some tea to the mums who haven't gone yet.' She pointed to several disconsolate groups huddled on the benches.

The younger girl nodded gratefully. 'As long as there's something I can do. Matron wouldn't let me go over and change—she said I was too late.'

Lynne went back to Dr Wishart. 'Only two possible plasters left for us, Doctor. They're on their last case in Casualty Theatre.'

'I don't know how Timothy managed when he's still so unfit.'

'Dr Gresham has taken over from him,' Lynne said with unexpected gentleness. 'Dr Layton has gone over to his room.'

She saw the other woman go very still. 'I must go to him—' she murmured half to herself.

'Dr Grant went with him. I think they'll give him a sedative,' Lynne reassured her. 'Sister Casualty said he was blaming himself for what happened.'

'So now he knows what it feels like.' Once again Sarah Wishart seemed to be speaking to herself.

Lynne was puzzled, but there was work still to be done. At long last they were finished. The ambulance men collected the children who were being allowed to go home. The parents had drifted away and the top lights had been switched off in the main hall. In the soft glow of side lamps there was little to show of what had been happening over the past few hours. Lynne could see Matron and Night Sister talking to Casualty Sister.

A somewhat familiar voice sounded just behind

Lynne's left ear. 'How about scrounging a mug of tea for your Uncle Ben? My crutches don't allow me to carry or fetch.'

Lynne swung round in surprise. 'I didn't hear you, Ben. It is nice to have you back, even on crutches.'

'Always willing to help out—besides, Sick Bay was dull and lonely. Why didn't you come back that night? There was enough beer for you.'

Lynne flushed in spite of her weariness. How silly her anger at Sarah Wishart seemed now. 'I'll get that tea.'

When she came back with a tray the centre bench appeared to have been pressed into service as a meeting place for weary staff. Even Matron and Night Sister accepted a cup, although the latter had to leave hers half finished and rush away in answer to a call from one of the wards.

Lynne saw Dr Wishart standing a little outside the group and took her a cup.

'Thanks, Nurse—Lynne,' she added shyly when she recognised the giver. 'Do you often have sessions like this?' She sank down on to the nearest bench and Lynne saw with concern how exhausted the woman looked. It was difficult to remember that she had been hating her for days.

Lynne sat down beside her. 'Not often—usually we share the load with the other hospitals. I expect it was because the school was practically on our doorstep that we got the lot.'

Sister Casualty was walking round to everyone now, thanking them and sending them off to bed. She came to Lynne. 'Staff Nurse, if you don't mind waiting a few moments.' The older woman moved on and Lynne saw her say something to Bibs, who was busy collecting up the empty cups like a lowly canteen volunteer.

'Isn't that Junior Staff?' Sarah Wishart asked suddenly.

Lynne nodded. 'She was out when the emergency call came,' she found herself defending Bibs.

'Bit of a man-chaser, isn't she?'

Lynne had to smile. 'That's why we call her dear Bibs—because she's always drooling over anyone in pants.'

Dr Wishart stood up abruptly as if she were no longer interested in local gossip. 'I must be off. I want to see if Doctor—Timothy—is all right.'

Lynne didn't bother to move. It had been fatal to sit down when she was so weary. 'He'll be all right.' She knew she sounded as if she were reassuring an anxious relative, but Sarah Wishart didn't appear to notice.

Lynne looked up to see Sister Casualty beckoning. Somehow she struggled to her feet. From somewhere her senior colleague had produced a fresh tray of tea and some sandwiches.

'Sit down, Staff Nurse, before you fall down, there's a good girl. Drink your tea and eat something first. We'll talk afterwards.'

Somewhere at the back of Lynne's mind she wondered vaguely why Sister Casualty had to talk at all. It did seem an odd time of day—or was it night? Obediently Lynne drank the hot sweet tea and discovered that she was hungry after all. At last she pushed away the half-empty plate and glanced up at Sister Casualty.

'Is something so very wrong, then, Sister?'

The older woman nodded. 'It's Junior Staff. I'm afraid she knew there had been an emergency call *before* she left the hospital.'

Lynne remembered Bibs' tearful face. 'She couldn't have, Sister. She asked me why I hadn't called her!'

Sister Casualty shook her head regretfully. 'The dining room maid gave her switchboard's message, and I'm sorry to say that Junior Staff went out of her way to be rude to the girl, who was so upset that she reported it to the canteen supervisior.'

'Oh no! If only I'd told you that I'd changed places on the rota,' Lynne said miserably, 'and I did tell her she needn't come back after second supper.'

'In which you exceeded even a deputy's authority,' Sister Casualty pointed out drily. 'However, that doesn't excuse the fact that Junior Staff did know about the emergency all staff recall and ignored it coldly and deliberately for the sake of a date.'

'But she did come back early,' Lynne tried once more.

'Only because Dr Grant had left a phone number and *he* was officially called back.' Sister Casualty sighed. 'It's unforgivable.'

Lynne remembered all her clashes with Bibs—the being locked in the sick bay storeroom, all the petty little digs—but they seemed such trifles now. 'Does Matron know?'

'Not yet. I happened to bump into the supervisor, but not knowing the circumstances I merely said I'd speak to Junior Staff.'

'Does Matron *have* to know?' Lynne heard the pleading note in her own voice with disbelief. 'I'm sure she's learned her lesson.'

Sister Casualty looked down at her desk. 'I didn't think you wanted the girl in the department after I retired,' she said almost casually.

Lynne flushed. 'Perhaps we had our differences,' she admitted, 'but not to the extent of having Matron transfer her for this.'

'It *is* a serious matter, but perhaps we can let it go this time. All right, Lynne, off you go to bed.'

Lynne walked very slowly along the corridor. As she

turned the corner she almost ran into the hurrying figure of Dr Wishart. She was startled to see how distressed the other woman seemed.

'I was just coming to fetch you. It's Timothy—he says he must see you right away.'

'I can't, it's out of bounds. If he were in the sick bay or back in Neuro it would be different.'

Sarah Wishart grabbed her by the arm. 'I'm not sending you on your own, you silly girl, I'm taking you! He's had a stiff sedative, but he's fighting it like mad. He says only you will know what he's talking about. Come on!'

Lynne saw the tears behind the anger and her objections died away. 'I'll do what I can.' She had no idea of what she might be letting herself in for, but there was obviously no chance of reaching her own bed until she complied.

The medical staff quarters were in semi-darkness and all seemed quiet until they turned the corner at the far end. Lynne could hear a moaning sound and then a low voice saying over and over again:

'Stop them—stop them!'

Sarah Wishart pushed open a door. 'Go in, Lynne, and do what you can. I'll stay here.'

Lynne hesitated, but the other woman gave her a nudge through the doorway and closed the door on her heels. There was a bedside lamp, and Lynne could make out the tossing figure of Timothy Layton. He was worse than that night on Neuro, Lynne thought grimly. Perhaps the same tactics would work now. She pulled up a chair and sat down and snatched at one of Timothy's flailing hands.

'Timothy, it's Lynne. Sarah said you had something to tell me.' She repeated the words several times before the man's eyes opened and he stared rather wildly at her.

'Oh, it's you, Lynne. I thought you were never coming. It's Tommy Jenkins—of course you know who he is.
It was his father trapped in that cave-in. He was at the
fire prevention class. I'm sure he went out just before
it all happened. You've got to see his mother for me
first thing. Tommy's either involved or he knows something. At first I thought he must have been trapped
in that terrible rush, but he couldn't have been. I
searched everywhere, I'm sure I did. Will you find out
for me, Lynne?'

Lynne held Timothy's hand firmly, her fingers strok-
ing his wrist soothingly. 'Of course I'll see Mrs Jenkins.
I'll catch her before she goes to work. Go to sleep,
Timothy.' There was no real need for her last words.
Already his eyes had closed and the wildness had gone
from his features.

After a few minutes Lynne gently disengaged her
fingers and stood up, almost crying out with the pain of
her stiffening muscles. The Casualty Officer never stirred as she opened the door. There was no sign of Sarah
Wishart, but Lynne didn't wait. She had done what she
had been asked to do and that was sufficient. She swayed
a little from sheer weariness and putting out a hand to
steady herself inadvertently pushed wider a door that
had been ajar. Here too a bedside lamp was on, but the
man lying sprawled on the bed was fast asleep. Ben
hadn't even bothered to undress and his crutches had
been flung into a corner. Without stopping to think
Lynne advanced into the room. She found an eiderdown
on the floor and gently placed it over the sleeping man.
How defenceless he looked as she tucked it around his
shoulders! He stirred suddenly and murmured something, but Lynne was too startled to linger. Hastily she
tiptoed out of the room and back to the swing door that
would let her out of forbidden territory. To her horror

she heard voices as she emerged. Too late she saw Night Sister talking to Dr Wishart.

Night Sister gave Lynne a hard look. 'You should have been in bed ages ago, Staff Nurse.'

'She was doing something for me, Night Sister,' Sarah Wishart broke in smoothly. 'Let me know if the child doesn't settle. I expect it's mostly remembered terror, poor little devil.'

Lynne waited until Night Sister had departed. 'Dr Layton is asleep now.'

'Thank God for that! I was afraid he was heading for a breakdown. What did he want?' She was woman enough to let unruly suspicion sharpen her voice.

Lynne hid a smile. So Sarah Wishart cared more than she was prepared to admit! 'I don't know why he couldn't tell you, unless it was because I know the people concerned. I said I'd see them in the morning.'

'You'll have to hurry—it's morning now,' Sarah Wishart said in such a light-hearted tone that Lynne glanced at her in astonishment.

The swing door was flung open with a crash and a heavy-eyed Ben emerged with a clatter of crutches. 'Can't you chattering females go to bed and let a chap sleep!'

'It might have helped if you undressed when you went to bed,' Lynne retorted, then went scarlet as both Ben Gresham and Sarah Wishart turned and stared at her.

The latter gave Lynne a little shove. 'Off you go to bed, Lynne. With luck you might get an hour before you go on your little errand.'

'Will someone kindly tell Uncle Ben what's going on?' Ben demanded gruffly.

Sarah Wishart took him firmly by the arm. 'Bed for you, young man. You're not back on the work rota yet. Thanks, Lynne, for seeing to Timothy.'

Lynne could feel Ben's gaze burning through her, but she didn't wait to explain. It was bad enough their guessing that she had been into Ben's room as well.

Lynne didn't bother going to bed. She had a long slow soak in the bath that took some of the nagging ache out of her spine. She slipped along to the little kitchenette and made herself some toast and strong coffee. She would put on a clean uniform and call at Mrs Jenkins' before she reported for duty.

Mrs Jenkins seemed startled when she opened the door to Lynne. 'Something wrong, Nurse? Has Mrs Leslie sent you?'

Lynne shook her head and followed the other woman into the kitchen. 'It was Dr Layton who sent me. He's worried about your Tommy.'

Mrs Jenkins almost slopped the cup of tea she was handing Lynne. 'Our Tommy? What about him? He's not ill—leastways he weren't when he went to bed. It's a mite early for him to be up as yet.'

Lynne wished she had more facts. Timothy had said so little for her to act on. 'It was about the accident at the school,' she said cautiously.

Mrs Jenkins nodded. 'Dreadful, wasn't it? I heard it on the late news. Ever so many kiddies trampled on. Thankful I was that Tommy got bored and came out early—said the doctor wasn't exactly exciting, like.' She flushed unhappily. 'Not meaning any disrespect, Nurse, seeing as how both of you saved my Roy.'

Lynne's heart sank. Tommy just could have been involved after all. 'Can I have a word with Tommy? It's rather important, Mrs Jenkins.'

Puzzled rather than anxious, Mrs Jenkins went to rouse her son. Lynne remembered Tommy as soon as the other woman returned with a tousled youngster in pyjamas still rubbing his eyes.

'What you getting me up in the middle of the night for, Mum? Oh, sorry, Nurse, I didn't understand it was for you. That bashed thumb of mine healed all right just as you said it would. What's it all about? Something wrong, like?'

Lynne picked her words carefully. 'Where did you go after you left Dr Layton's talk last night?'

Tommy wrinkled up his brow. 'Me and George kicked a ball about for a bit and then went over to the park. Some kids were larking about on racing bikes. We made them give us a go. I guess we headed for home after that.'

'When did you know about the accident at the school?' Lynne felt she was on safer ground now.

Tommy flashed her a look. 'Not until it was too late to see the fun. George's brother came to fetch him home. He said there'd been dozens of ambulances, but the police wouldn't let him close enough to have a good look.'

Lynne made one final attempt. 'When you and George slipped out of the lecture room were you the only ones?'

'Naw—about six or seven, maybe. We got bored, see.'

Lynne stood up dispiritedly. 'Then you couldn't have seen anyone touch the box of smoke bombs—'

A sudden move from Tommy made her jump. 'Didn't see nobody, Nurse. All right if I get some more shut-eye, Mum?'

Mrs Jenkins looked at Lynne worriedly. 'You're not thinking he's mixed up in that dreadful business, Nurse?'

Lynne shook her head. 'Dr Layton only thought he might have seen something, that's all.'

'Leave it with me, Nurse. If our Tommy knows I'll get to the bottom of it. Was any of the kiddies killed, like?'

Lynne smiled reassuringly. 'No, thank heaven. Bad as

it was it could have been much worse.' She shuddered a little, remembering last night. It was always worse when children were involved—they seemed so helpless some-how. 'I must go, Mrs Jenkins. Thanks for the tea.'

Lynne was breathless by the time she reached Casu-alty. Talking to Tommy had taken her longer than she had expected.

Sister Casualty was sitting in her little office staring down at the morning papers. Black headlines screamed out the facts: CHILDREN CRUSHED IN MOCK FIRE PANIC: ENQUIRY ORDERED: WHO WAS RESPONSIBLE? There was much more and photo-graphs of upturned benches and ambulance men and the limp bodies of unconscious children.

Sister Casualty glanced up as Lynne came. 'I don't know which is worse—being there when it happens, or dealing with the consequences. I wonder what actually happened. Do you suppose Dr Layton was too realistic with his demonstration?'

'Someone set off the smoke bomb outside the lecture room—Dr Layton hadn't even touched the box,' Lynne said without thinking.

'Indeed! You seem to have inside information, Staff Nurse. Perhaps that's why there have been some phone calls for you already. I trust you haven't been talking unwisely to reporters as well.' Then she noticed Lynne's startled face and chuckled a little. 'All right, Lynne. It was Dr Wishart who phoned. She'll be in the dining room. I don't suppose an extra break will do you any harm. Sorry I couldn't give you the morning off. I don't suppose we'll have a major episode *three* days in a row!'

Blast Sarah Wishart, but of course Timothy would want to know what she had found out. The locum Junior Casualty Officer was sitting alone when Lynne went in.

Her pale face flushed a little when she saw the staff nurse.

'Sorry to have to bother you like this, Lynne, but Timothy said he'd get up if I didn't find out whether you'd had any luck.'

'I don't think Tommy knows anything, but he did say several other boys left when he did. Tommy and his mate George don't appear to have been on the school premises when anything happened.'

'Are you sure?' Sarah Wishart's voice was curt.

Lynne ignored the tone. 'I don't think wild horses could have kept the boys away from the *fun*—his word, not mine—if he'd had an inkling. He only knew *afterwards* from George's brother, and *he* wasn't able to get close enough.'

'Then Timothy doesn't have any real evidence that someone outside the classroom was responsible for the panic. He's got to know. The papers are trying to crucify him, I know they will!'

'But he must know where the first smoke came from,' Lynne insisted.

'From the ventilators,' said a bright voice, and they both turned as Ben Gresham stomped into the dining room, his crutches making a cheerful clatter. 'Hello, Lynne, don't you work in Casualty any more?'

'I asked her to come up, Ben. Sit down and tell us how you know about the ventilators?'

'I asked Timothy, of course. He was going on and on about the accident and the only way to shut him up was to ask sensible questions and make him think constructively. Any luck, Lynne?'

'Tommy wasn't there, but other boys could have been,' Lynne said slowly. 'His mother thinks she can get to the bottom of it.'

'Well, if she can't the insurance investigators will.

They'll be able to decide where things started,' Ben said firmly.

'But what about the papers?' Sarah and Lynne demanded in unison.

'Speculation—nothing more. You read through the reports carefully and you'll find that no one accuses Timothy of anything. The school authorities have more to worry about than he has.'

'I wish you'd drum that into Timothy's head,' Sarah Wishart said disconsolately.

'I have, and I think if you'll take him over a large tray of breakfast he'll eat it. You'll have to hurry or he'll be getting dressed to fetch it himself!'

Ben poured a second cup of coffee and pushed it towards Lynne. 'Drink it, little one. It's not very often I have you for breakfast.' He seemed a little shy and glanced at Lynne doubtfully. 'Did I dream it or did you tuck me in?'

Lynne hung her head. 'I thought you were asleep!'

He chuckled. 'I thought I was dreaming, but now I know it was for real. How come you were in my room?'

But Lynne only gulped down her coffee. 'I've got to go. It was an accident, in any case.' She reached the door before Ben recovered sufficiently to call after her, 'It was a lovely accident, then!'

Lynne was glad to get back to the quiet routine of Casualty.

'Sister's gone to give her report to Matron.' Bibs sounded so subdued that Lynne looked at her sharply.

'Oh, you mean about the accident cases—' and then she stopped.

'So you know then?' the other girl asked in such a low voice that Lynne had to strain her ears to catch the words. 'It was a damn fool thing to do, but every single time I had a date with Peter something turned up to stop it. I couldn't risk it happening again—he might have thought I wasn't interested enough.'

Lynne was tempted to tease her, but she only said gently, 'But it's all right now, isn't it?'

'Sister didn't say who stood up for me, but it must have been you. There isn't anyone else who would have.' The younger girl seemed embarrassed, but she went on bravely, 'I guess Peter and I have you to thank that I wasn't sent packing.'

Lynne recovered a little of her own composure. 'I'm glad things are working out all right.' It sounded horribly stiff and stilted.

Bibs hesitated again and then plunged. 'And it was only meant as a joke that time we locked you in. I told Peter you could get out another way—'

Lynne had to laugh. 'You had me so muddled I didn't know *what* was happening! Let's forget about it, eh?'

'All right by me. I'm glad you and Ben have made it up. I told him you were soft on old Timothy and he swallowed it like a babe.'

Part of Lynne went cold inside. It was all very well for Bibs to assume that *all* her mischief was undone. She only wished she could be as sure herself. She couldn't imagine that someone who kept referring to himself as Uncle Ben was interested in a stronger relationship. Suddenly she felt utterly drained and weary, and she was thankful when the phone rang and she could hurry away. It was just as well she hadn't known the extent of Bibs' machinations when she had pleaded for the girl. Her affairs were getting more muddled every moment. She couldn't even have the comfort of talking things over with Timothy Layton. It looked as if everything was working out for other people, but not for herself.

To Lynne's astonishment it was her mother on the line. 'Lynne dear, I thought I'd better tell you before you heard it on the news. It—'

'Mum, what's wrong? Is it Dad?'

'Of course not, Lynne—whatever gave you such an idea! It's Aunt Jenny. She's had an accident, somewhere in France—I can't pronounce the name of the wretched place. Your father's taking the noon ferry. There's too much fog to fly and they sounded pretty worried about her. It isn't as if Jenny has any relatives—'

Lynne found the strength from somewhere to sympathise with her mother, even to feel sorry for her godmother—after all, they had had some good times together. Timothy would be upset. Then she remembered Aunt Jenny's suggestion. Why, they could have been in France together!

She pulled herself together. 'Is there anything I can do, Mum?'

'Nothing at the moment, dear. I expect you're kept pretty busy. Get over when you can. 'Bye.'

Lynne put down the phone. She had never felt more remote from her parents. They would have heard the news—even read the papers—but it wouldn't have occurred to them that their daughter would be concerned in any part of last night's tragic happenings at a local school. The tunnel cave-in had been different. Thanks to TV they couldn't overlook their daughter's involvement. She sighed and went back to her work. She must remember to tell Timothy. She wondered if he had had a premonition about her godmother's accident. He seemed to have been afraid that tragedy was threatening.

It seemed Lynne's day for phone calls. It was Mrs Jenkins this time and she seemed in quite a state. 'I was that upset when I heard the news, Nurse. Do you think she wants anything sent?'

It was a moment or two before Lynne realised that

Mrs Jenkins was talking about her godmother. She reassured her. 'My father's gone to France. He'll let you know if there's anything, Mrs Jenkins.' She braced herself to the next question. 'Have you got anything out of Tommy?'

There was a pause at the other end of the line. 'I'll have you know my Tommy's not concerned in any way, Nurse!'

Lynne rushed to put things right. 'I know he isn't, Mrs Jenkins. It's only because I'm concerned about Dr Layton—'

'Sorry I went off like that, Nurse; specially since you've been so good to us. The school's closed for a fortnight—gives the kids time to get over it, like. But one thing struck me as odd—two of the mothers been round to see me, asking me if Tommy knew where their boys had got to.'

'Can you give me their names, Mrs Jenkins?' Lynne interrupted.

'Doesn't seem right somehow. It isn't as if we knows they had anything to do with it. Could be they were afraid their kids had been hurt and they not notified. I told them to check with the hospital. The boys could have gone off for any number of reasons—you know what kids are these days.'

Lynne heard Sister Casualty's familiar footsteps. 'I must go now, Mrs Jenkins.'

'Right you are, Nurse. I'll keep you posted if I hears anything.'

'Anything for us, Staff Nurse?'

Lynne shook her head. 'My godmother's cleaning woman, Sister.' She explained about the accident in France.

Sister Casualty sat down heavily. 'Whoever said life was dull and ordinary?' she demanded of no one in particular. 'By the way, Matron was very impressed by your handling of things last night.'

Lynne blushed. 'We'd had plenty of practice, Sister.'

'So you have—I sometimes wonder if Casualty is the right place for younger nurses. I know they have to have the training some time. I'm not even sure that it's the right place for you, Lynne. It's all right for someone like me. When one's older one's worked out some sort of philosophy that makes it bearable.'

Lynne stood very still. 'You mean that you and Matron have changed your minds about my taking over, Sister?'

The older woman smiled a little. 'Nothing like that— far from it! I was only thinking my doubts out loud.'

'Any tea going for a thirsty invalid, Sister?' Ben appeared in the doorway grinning cheekily at them.

'We never heard your crutches,' Lynne said rather stupidly.

'Simple, because I've handed them back. I've been scientifically strapped up now and told to walk on my foot regardless of whether it hurts like blazes or not. With old Timothy temporarily on the sick list again and Dr Wishart walking about in a dream I thought you might like my assistance. As long as you don't want me to run anywhere I'll manage.'

Sister Casualty chuckled. 'Better get some cups of tea from the canteen lady, Staff Nurse. I haven't heard any ambulances lately.'

'Ssh, Sister! Don't tempt them.' Ben held up two hands with fingers crossed.

Lynne felt positively light-hearted as she went across to the canteen window. There weren't many people sitting on the benches and most of them regulars coming up for their daily dressings—varicose veins, old injuries, plaster casts for trimming. They greeted her with a cheery smile or a teasing word. There was nothing that Bibs and the juniors couldn't manage.

Lynne stopped to steady the cups outside the office door and then she heard Sister Casualty's voice raised a little:

'I wouldn't tell her, Dr Gresham. It isn't as if you're in a position to do anything about it. Casualty Sister is an important post and don't you forget it, young man!'

Very quietly Lynne put the tray down on a table and hurriedly went towards the linen room—the traditional refuge of all nurses who wanted to cry, or just to be alone.

# CHAPTER TEN

At long last Lynne lifted her damp cheek from the cool pile of sheets. As she fished for a handkerchief a hand from nowhere, it seemed, proffered her a large man-sized one. She mopped her eyes hastily and stared crossly at Ben, who was sitting quite calmly on the pair of steps the nurses used for getting at the top shelves.

'How long have you been here, Ben Gresham?' Lynne demanded, furious at being caught in a rare moment of weakness.

'Let's see, I rescued a tray of tea from outside Sister's office. We drank ours and then I came to look for you. Yours is getting rather cold, I'm afraid.'

'How did you know where I'd be?' Lynne was less heated now. Ben's manner was so matter-of-fact that she would have got nowhere trying to pick a quarrel.

'Well, you could have been in the sluice, but I thought the linen room more likely. Dear Bibs always comes here when she's upset.'

Lynne remembered the time she had caught the pair of them here. 'You can have your handkerchief back,' and she thrust it at him.

'I thought heroines always washed and ironed them tenderly before returning them,' Ben teased her gently.

'You've been reading the wrong books!' Lynne snapped. 'I must get back to work. Sister will wonder where I am.' She tried to push past him, but Ben held her firmly.

'Sister's got a Hospital Management Committee meeting—an emergency one,' Ben retorted calmly. 'There's nothing the rest of the staff can't handle. Now suppose you tell me why you were crying?'

'It's none of your business—let me go!'

'Not until you tell me, Lynne, and I don't care how long I have to wait for an answer. And it is *my* business. Since the tray of tea was just outside Sister's office you must have heard or seen something that upset you. Since I didn't see you or hear you, we must have been discussing something important. Let's think—oh yes, I was saying that no department or person in a hospital is indispensable. The work can always be done by someone else, or somewhere else for that matter. Sister Casualty got quite hot under the collar. She insisted that Casualty was the front line for any situation and that her post was in fact more actively important than Matron's—in an emergency situation, of course.'

Lynne stared at him belligerently. 'Then what weren't you to tell me?'

Ben put back his head and laughed. 'So that's it—I might have known! Since when are you the Matron of St David's, eh?'

Lynne had to join in his laughter and suddenly she felt much better. But Ben wasn't finished.

'You're not going to tell me that's the only reason you were crying, Lynne? There has to be *something* else or someone. Is it Timothy?' His face had gone very serious.

Before Lynne could answer there was a timid knock on the door and the voice of one of the juniors:

'Staff Nurse, two cases have come in and there's another being unloaded from the ambulance.'

'Coming!' This time Ben Gresham made no attempt to stop Lynne's passage.

By lunch-time they were back in business with a normal intake of casualties. It was Lynne's half day, so she would be going to second lunch. Dr Wishart came

out of Casualty Theatre just as she was leaving the
department.

'Staff Nurse, Sister says you have a half day. Could
you spare a little time to see Timothy?'

Lynne halted reluctantly. She longed to be free of
involvement with anyone. She felt emotionally drained
and so tired after last night that she could have started
crying again—this time for no reason at all.

'All right, Dr Wishart, if you think it will help. How is
he?' she asked so politely that the other woman smiled a
little.

'To think that I lost sleep over you!' she murmured
half to herself. 'He's better, thank goodness, but I think
he needs to hear anything you know—in person. I don't
know why, but he seems to feel that I'm keeping something back.'

Without stopping to think, Lynne said swiftly, 'You're
right, he does, but not about anything that's happened
now. He wants to know why you walked out of his life all
those years ago!' She went scarlet, but managed to look
Sarah Wishart squarely in the face.

The older woman had gone very pale. 'You don't
know what you're talking about! You can't!'

'If you mean the facts—you're right, I don't. However, I do know that whatever happened left Timothy
Layton a very lonely man.' She lifted a hand to silence
the other's protest. 'You forget, I was with him that
night after he'd had the blow on the head when he
thought I was you.'

But Sarah Wishart wasn't really listening to Lynne any
more. 'If only he'd told me!—but then he always was
so shy.'

Lynne waited another minute and then slipped away.
If Dr Wishart still wanted her to talk to Timothy she
would be in the dining room or the Nurses' Home. One

thing she knew—she wouldn't be going out today.

It must have been teatime when Lynne roused from a heavy but refreshing sleep. The sun was shining and the wind had dropped. It was too late in the year to call it the traditional 'little summer', but it was a bonus day all the same. She would get dressed and go for a long brisk walk—stop for tea somewhere. She might even go home this evening and try to bring back a trace of normality to her muddled-up life. Her mother was bound to have news of Aunt Jenny.

Lynne was never quite sure when she became aware that she was being followed. First it had been when she was walking along the side of the road—a car that drove very slowly and then whizzed past her. She was sure it had come past her more than once. It was light-coloured—it could be an unwashed white. Lynne had instinctively turned off the road on to one of the paths crossing the heath. There were clumps of shrubbery ahead and once there she could glance back without being noticed. She *was* right—there was someone following her, someone who was breathing heavily and stumbling often. Lynne was about to take to her heels in sheer panic when a voice shouted out:

'Lynne! For God's sake, wait for a chap!' Then there was the sound of someone falling.

Lynne swung round in time to see Ben sprawl full length. She ran to him anxiously. 'Ben! Are you all right? Why didn't you say it was you?'

Ben lifted himself up on one elbow. 'Chance is a fine thing! My ankle isn't a hundred per cent yet, you know.'

Lynne squatted down on her heels beside him. 'Then it was you following me—and in that white car as well?'

Ben hauled himself up into a sitting position. 'Whew! That ground is harder than it looks. To answer your question—I certainly didn't fly from St David's, I can tell you. Sarah lent me her car—mine is in dock and she's too busy with Timothy to want it, for one thing.'

Lynne listened with a puzzled expression. 'Then why did you sail past me?'

Ben glanced down rather sheepishly. 'You could say I was trying to pluck up enough courage to break into your obvious wish for solitude. You did rather brush me off in the linen cupboard, you know!'

Lynne tried to feign indifference. 'Did I? I had to deal with those cases.'

'Once upon a time we would have tackled them together,' Ben suggested. 'However, someone else answered my question about Timothy—two people, in fact.'

Lynne stared at him in bewilderment. 'I haven't a clue to what you're talking about,' she stated flatly.

'Perhaps it was all in my own mind,' Ben admitted. 'I'd got it into my head that you were gone on old Timothy. It seemed that every time I looked for you his affairs got in the way. It never occurred—'

'—to you that he might be talking to me because I reminded him of the woman he loved or that every time I wanted to have a word with—'

'—me, I was always involved with someone else. I don't suppose you realised that I was doing it for the same reasons!'

Lynne stared at Ben, her eyes wide with disbelief. 'I don't believe it!'

Ben reached out a long arm and pulled her to him and kissed her with lingering satisfaction before releasing her. 'Well, do you believe your Uncle Ben now?'

Lynne smiled down at him. 'I don't usually kiss my uncle like this.' This time she bent and kissed him until passion leapt between them like a summer storm.

Ben's voice was shaky when he finally disengaged himself. 'Steady on, Lynne—remember the state of my health!'

'I thought it was only a wrenched ankle!' Lynne teased him. She helped him to his feet. 'Hadn't we better get back to the car? I was looking for somewhere to have tea. I'm famished!'

Ben pretended to lean on her heavily. 'I'm too love-sick to eat a thing! Honestly, Lynne, couldn't you have let a fellow know sooner?'

Lynne adjusted his arm more comfortably across her shoulder. 'How could I? I didn't know myself. As a matter of fact I thought Sister Casualty was warning you off—that's why I ran off to cry.'

Ben chuckled. 'Perhaps she was, in an oblique kind of way. She may be afraid that her retirement would be affected if we get married—'

'If? I didn't even know you'd asked me!' Lynne retorted.

'Suppose you learn to allow me to finish my sentences, young lady. I was about to add if we get married before Easter.'

Lynne paused to let Ben lean against Sarah's car and swung round to face him. 'If you want us to have a decent honeymoon we'd have to work it in before then. Sister Casualty will have to relieve me for that fortnight!'

'Oh, Lynne darling, those are the nicest words I've heard for a long time! I take it you intend to work after we're married, then?'

Lynne looked up at him a trifle anxiously. 'I hope you won't disapprove, Ben—I don't want to let Matron down, at least not yet. It means I can work with you every day.'

'Most days,' Ben agreed. 'Oh, I forgot, you don't know. Timothy's going back to university teaching as

Sarah's got herself a job in medical research starting at Easter. It means I have a reasonable chance of moving up to Senior Casualty Officer. With the new pay scales it means you can stop work any time we decide to start a family.'

Lynne went pink. 'Suppose I want to be a working mother?' she teased.

Ben chuckled. 'Suppose we decide that when the time comes, sweetheart! How about finding that tea place? I've recovered my appetite twice over!'

Lynne snuggled down beside Ben as he started up the car. 'It all seems too wonderful to be true. Oh, before I forget, remind me to ring Mother before we go back.'

Ben chuckled. 'You want me inspected so soon?'

'It wasn't that at all!' Lynne protested. 'I want to find out about Aunt Jenny.'

There was a dismayed sound from Ben. 'Oh, lord, I should have told you before, but I got sidetracked a bit.'

'Is it—bad news, then?' Lynne shivered a little. A moment ago she had been so happy, and already someone's trouble was impinging upon it.

''Fraid so. I didn't speak to whoever phoned, but apparently she never recovered consciousness. Oh, and I was to tell you that the crash occurred when she tried to avoid running down a child who'd darted out into the road. They thought you might like to know.'

'Poor Aunt Jenny—and she never had any of her own,' Lynne said soberly. 'Let's have that tea. I need a cuppa badly. She was very good to me in her own way.'

'And to Timothy, and to me as well, I suppose, but she wasn't the sort of person you could get very close to.'

Lynne pointed suddenly. 'There's a teashop. I think she kept people at arm's length after her husband died. I don't know the details.'

The tea was hot and strong and the scones freshly

made and the cake looked the home variety as well.

'You're in luck, Ben—no mingy portions here. They must have known we were coming!'

The woman who was serving them smiled suddenly. 'From the hospital, aren't you? Thought I recognised your face, Nurse—I saw it on the telly when there was that poor fellow trapped. Was you there too, Doctor? Seems as how I knows your face as well.'

'Could be, if you've been up to Casualty. I remember now, you scalded your arm, didn't you?' Ben was glad when she left them to eat their tea. 'We might as well wear labels, St David's brand, and be done with it. Oh, I saw Sarah before I came out. Of course you know that, since we've got her car. Timothy wants me to be best man and she wonders if you'd be her bridesmaid—says she owes you such a lot. Funny how I thought you two hated one another's guts at one time.'

'Just a simple misunderstanding,' Lynne murmured. 'More tea, Ben?'

'Please, darling. What kind of ring would you like? Oh, by the way, Timothy and Sarah would like us to look in when we get back.'

'Which answer do you want first, Ben? Tea and a sapphire and did Timothy and Sarah know you were going to ask me?' Lynne said all in a rush.

'Steady on, girl! I didn't even know that myself until I fell down on the heath and you were kind enough to turn back to my rescue. Maybe I got the love bug from Sarah and Timothy. No, that's not right. I've been in love with you for a long time, but you never gave a sign that you cared twopence for anything other than your career.'

'You mean you're begrudging me any ambition already?' Lynne demanded in mock anger.

But Ben didn't rise to the bait. 'Not a bit of it, provided you put me fairly high among your priorities.

I'd be a fool to deny that your salary will help us set up home all the sooner. I'm not quite sure whether the post of Senior Casualty Officer carries with it an option to live out. If I only have to spend my on call nights here it won't be so bad.'

—'Or we might even find something close enough.' Lynne suddenly remembered Aunt Jenny, but she didn't say anything. It would be too ghoulish to speculate when the poor woman was scarcely dead.


Timothy Layton and Sarah Wishart were in the Common Room sitting in front of the fire. There was no one else about when Lynne and Ben walked in.

Sarah took one look at their faces. 'I see that congratulations are in order for you two as well,' she said softly.

Lynne could scarcely believe her eyes. Timothy looked ten years younger and all signs of strain had vanished. As for Sarah, the harshness had gone from her features and from her manner. Even her red hair had taken on a softer glow.

Timothy looked from Sarah to Lynne. 'It's hard to believe you two aren't related. You could be sisters.'

'All in your imagination, Timothy old boy—nothing but the colour of their hair. Where's that celebration drink got to?' Ben put in swiftly, but the two women only exchanged smiles—they knew what Timothy meant.

Ben and Sarah were called back to Casualty just before supper, but insisted that Lynne waited with Timothy—they wouldn't be long.

Timothy chuckled at that. 'Seems we've all heard that before! Don't go, Lynne. There are some things I'd like to ask you. I understand that your godmother is dead.'

Lynne nodded. She was remembering what she had said to Sarah and was feeling a trifle uncomfortable.

Timothy didn't seem to expect an answer. 'Sarah has told me what happened—with John, I mean. There was never any question of their running away together—they weren't in love or anything like that. They worked in the same department, but on different lines of research. When Jenny used to get hysterical if he even looked at another woman he went to ask Sarah's advice, nothing more. The time of the accident she wasn't even in the car—John had borrowed it. He'd been drinking rather heavily and didn't bother to ask. Sarah was away at a meeting and when she got back the whole place was buzzing. Jenny had put it out that John had left a note saying he was going off with Sarah, but no one ever saw it. Sarah was too upset to defend herself and disappeared without a word. She says she didn't know I cared so much—'

'And now she does. I'm so glad for you, Timothy,' Lynne said softly.

Timothy smiled back. 'Thanks to you—and I'm so glad you and Ben have got together at last. I couldn't see you getting old as Sister Casualty, somehow.'

'I'm still taking the job,' Lynne pointed out.

'Family permitting, eh!' Timothy chuckled. 'Good old Mother Nature, she'll look after the ifs and the buts. Good lord, they *are* back already!'

Sarah and Ben were wearing a very triumphant air. 'We've got it all worked out. Whichever pair gets married first, the other acts as best man and bridesmaid—and then vice versa. We should be able to work in the honeymoons as well.'

'Not unless you want to do all the Casualty work yourself, Ben,' Timothy pointed out. 'I'm marrying the locum, not you. We can have ours after we leave St David's. The university won't need us until the end of the Easter holiday. You getting married in white,

Lynne? Then Ben and I can book our morning suits for both dates.'

'Make it three dates,' said a voice from behind them. They turned to see Peter Grant grinning at them. 'Yes, Barbara has said yes.'

For a moment they all stared until Lynne remembered. 'So dear old Bibs will now be Barbara Grant— look after her, Peter. She needs a lot of loving.'

There was a startled gasp and too late Lynne realised that Bibs had been standing behind Peter Grant all the time. But it didn't seem to matter. Timothy produced a bottle of champagne by some magic and they all drank one another's health. They were late going in to supper, but for once the maids didn't seem to mind and there was a little humming going on in the background that sounded remarkably like the Wedding March.

It was late when Ben escorted Lynne back to the Nurses' Home. He gave her a swift kiss. 'I'll be glad when we have our own place. There's too much sharing going on at the moment. 'I'm going to get my dates in first. I can't have the youngsters getting in ahead of us!' Reluctantly he released her. 'When are you off tomorrow? So we can go shopping for the ring.'

'I'm off until eleven, but isn't that too early for you, Ben?'

He gave her hand a squeeze. 'Not on an occasion like buying a ring for my girl. Listen, sweetheart, I'm not rushing you too fast, am I? You haven't even told me that you love me!'

Lynne lifted her face. 'Kiss me and you'll know the answer, Ben darling!'

There was a sudden blaze of headlights and a car horn hooted and the two of them sprang apart.

'It's as bad as being in Piccadilly Circus,' Ben said ruefully. 'We'll have to do something about this goodnight business tomorrow.'

'I'm on call,' Lynne reminded him.

Ben grinned. 'That makes two of us. Meet you in the linen cupboard at eight o'clock.'

It was so absurd that Lynne was laughing as she walked into the front hall of the Nurses' Home. She never noticed the juniors waiting to phone.

'Another good staff nurse we're losing,' one said gloomily.

'She may stay on for a bit. They say Bibs is getting hitched at last.'

'About time—she's been hunting a long time. I wonder who we'll get instead.'

'Never mind, it will be our turn to be staff nurses one of these days and we'll be nice to juniors. What do *you* want? Students have to use the other phone!'

Lynne, remembering that she hadn't phoned home, came back just in time to catch the last remark. She only smiled when they insisted that she use the phone first. Things didn't change so much after all.

Her mother sounded rather subdued. 'Your father won't be back until tomorrow. There are some formalities to be seen to—you know how it is. What time will he be back? In time for supper if the traffic's not too heavy. Sorry, I didn't catch what you said. You want to bring Ben home—why?'

Lynne was suddenly shy. 'Because we'd like to show you the ring. I couldn't tell you before. I only knew myself this afternoon. Wedding? Easter—I've remembered they don't like you marrying in Lent. Look after yourself, Mum.'

Lynne was chuckling to herself as she came out of the kiosk. At least her mother wouldn't be feeling lonely tonight—she'd be too busy phoning all the relatives.

'We wish you every happiness, Staff Nurse,' the two juniors said shyly.

Lynne blushed as she thanked them. Love was beginning to seem a very public affair.

Lynne needn't have worried about telling Sister Casualty. The hospital grapevine had been only too busy. 'Love seems to be like the measles—everyone's catching it,' the older woman said drily. 'Three weddings in the department—no one's mind will be on work for a single moment. I wish you every happiness, Lynne. Your young man informs me that you'll be taking over from me as planned. It's nice to know that I can still retire! How about letting me see the ring?'

A trifle shyly Lynne unpinned it from her watch pocket and placed it in her colleague's palm.

Sister Casualty looked at it thoughtfully. 'That would have been two years' salary in my day. You young people don't know how lucky you are.'

Lynne was startled to see the other woman brush away a tear with an angry gesture. It was beginning to seem that everyone had their soft streak, the point at which they could cry.

Sister Casualty handed back the ring. 'I'd better have a chat with Matron. It looks as if we're going to have some staff changes. I'll miss Dr Wishart—she *was* a woman with no nonsense about her, or so I thought!'

Lynne's parents gave Ben such a warm welcome that she was ashamed of her doubts. Perhaps the gap between them had been as much her fault as theirs.

Mr Howard chuckled when he saw his wife produce some lists. 'Come and have a beer in the kitchen, Ben. This is where the women take charge.'

Lynne, feeling a little deserted, turned back to her mother. 'Mum, we want to keep things simple.'

Mrs Howard didn't appear to hear her daughter. 'I've

made a rough list of names. It should work out at about a hundred and fifty at the church and somewhere near a hundred for the reception. I expect you'll want to ask some of the nurses. Now about bridesmaids—'

Lynne plunged in, 'I want Sarah Wishart, and one's enough, Mum.'

Mrs Howard stared at her daughter. 'Sarah? Is she one of your set? I suppose we can have her, but you must have Letty and Jane and I think Douglas is old enough to be a pageboy—he'll look sweet in a kilt with the girls in Swiss muslin—they have some lovely ones now. What's Sarah's colouring?'

Lynne made one more attempt. 'Sarah's red-headed like me and her fiancé, Timothy Layton's, to be best man. Mum, we don't want a big wedding!'

Her father appeared with a tray of drinks. 'You might as well give in gracefully, Lynne. Your mother's only got one chick to get wed, so it's this wedding or nothing.'

Ben gave Lynne a sympathetic grin. 'We don't want to cause a lot of trouble, Mrs Howard, honestly.'

Mrs Howard accepted a sherry from her husband. 'I'll take Lynne to be measured for her dress and we can choose samples for the bridesmaids' frocks. Ben, you and Lynne must make out a guest list as far as your relatives and special friends at the hospital are concerned. Then there's a gift list—we can organise it with one of the big stores so you won't end up with twenty cheese-boards.' She slowed down for a moment and held up her glass. 'Happiness to you both, my dears.'

Mr Howard fought to get a word in. 'What family have you, Ben? We'd like to arrange a get-together before the wedding.'

Ben shook his head. 'I'm afraid I've only got an older brother out in Australia, and I doubt if he could get back—it's a busy time for him. He's a cattle rancher. My parents died a few years back.'

With a slight feeling of shock Lynne realised how little she knew about the man she loved—except that she loved him, of course. It had all happened so quickly in one sense. Yet in another she felt she had known him for years. They had both crammed so much experience into the many emergency situations in Casualty. They had shared horror and grief, and relief and even joy when things turned out better than anyone had dared to hope. They had also shared laughter and tears, heartbreak and new-found love. Lynne moved quickly to Ben's side and slipped her hand into his.

Ben smiled at her as much as to say: 'Let them get on with it. As long as we end up married the way there doesn't matter.'

Lynne squeezed his fingers to show she understood. A few fittings, a few lists—and the wedding day, of course, but the rest of the time she and Ben would be busy in their own safe world in Casualty.

Later, Lynne's father drew her to one side. 'I don't know whether your mother has had time to tell you, but Aunt Jenny left you the house. As you know, the bottom flat is rented out to the old couple. There's also some money in investments that's partly tied up in an educational trust for any children you and Ben may have, but there will be a nice little nest egg for you as well. If Ben has to move to another hospital too far away for travelling you can always rent it under some arrangement where you and Ben can move back in—a six months' lease or something like that. We can arrange it with her solicitor.'

Lynne was silent for a moment. 'Do you think she had a premonition or something?'

Mr Howard shrugged his shoulders. 'Who can say? I don't think she had been very happy since John died and lately she had seemed worried about something. I'm afraid we haven't seen much of her these past few months, apart from that dinner.'

Ben came to join them. 'I think we should be getting back, Lynne. It's been a busy day.'

Lynne glanced down at her very new ring. 'And a very exciting one!'

'Surely you're not going yet?' Mrs Howard protested.

'Sorry, Mum, but we're really on call. Sarah and Bibs are standing in for us.'

'All these names—and I never can understand how you still have to work even though you've done a full shift or whatever you call it,' Mrs Howard murmured.

Lynne kissed her mother. 'Never mind, Mum—we don't always understand it ourselves. We only get called out in big emergencies—more than the night staff can cope with. Goodnight, Dad.'

'Wait a minute, Lynne. When can you come with me about your dress?'

'On my next day off—it isn't as if there's a terrific rush. It's still months away. Let us get used to being engaged first!'

'Time goes quicker than you think. All right, ring me when you know your day off. Take good care of her, Ben. She's the only one we have.'

Then they were safely outside the door and getting into Sarah's car. 'Whew! Weddings mean more fuss than I bargained for—good thing I love you so much. Your mother was telling me about your godmother's leaving us the place. How do you feel about it, my love?'

'Can we think about it tomorrow?' Lynne pleaded. 'I only want to think about us tonight!'

'Suits me. Where do you want to go, sweetheart?'

Lynne glanced at him in astonishment. 'I thought we had to go straight back.'

Ben shook his head. 'Sarah said there was no reason to worry about rushing back.'

'But, Ben, they might be busy!'

'And they might be when we're on again, sweetheart. This is a good chance to practise putting me first,' Ben teased her gently. 'How about driving up over the downs? We might also get in some kissing practice as well!'

All the world seemed to have had the same idea, but at last they found a gateway away from everyone else. They sat quiet with their arms round one another and looked down on the galaxy of lights that made up one of man's cities.

'It looks so peaceful,' Lynne murmured, and snuggled down on Ben's shoulder.

He held her very close. 'Lynne darling, I never knew I could be so happy.'

'Me neither.'

The moon had dipped below the horizon by the time they left the quiet hillside and headed back towards St David's. It was a night that neither of them would ever forget—a night to cherish against the next major emergency in Casualty.

Lynne had never known time to rush by so quickly. It seemed to affect the whole of the department. Of course it wasn't every day that five members of Casualty staff got engaged—six if one included Peter Grant on a part-time basis. At least the Ward Sisters knew where to ring first if they required him urgently!

Even Sister Casualty appeared to be caught up in the stream of happiness that seemed to make the work progress on silken wheels. She coaxed Bibs into contacting an uncle who was persuaded that giving away a niece he scarcely knew was an important family duty.

She insisted on helping the girl with her plans and seemed to know a surprising amount about organising weddings, receptions, and even honeymoons.

Bibs went round wearing an expression of happy disbelief and hadn't scolded a junior for days. 'I didn't know people could be so wonderful,' she told Lynne, and there could have been a glint of tears in her eyes. 'Sister has even helped us to find a small flat. I know Peter has to live in, officially, but at least we'll have a place we can call our own. How about you?'

Lynne sighed. 'It seems to be the decorators—we decided we wanted a lot of light colours. Odd how big it makes the rooms seem. We've got to get rid of some of the furniture as we want some things of our own. Mum and Dad are insisting on giving us the bedroom suite—' She fell silent, remembering her visit with Ben to the empty house.

At least it wasn't quite empty. The old couple were still downstairs, but as Ben pointed out, church mice couldn't have been quieter. Mrs Jenkins was hovering about with an expression half of outrage that anyone should touch her late mistress's things and half curiosity about Ben's and Lynne's plans. Mrs Leslie had left her a small legacy, but as Mrs Jenkins pointed out:

'I'd still like to keep my hand in, what with prices going up and all. I'd be willing to give you a special price, like.'

Lynne had reassured her, 'We'll let you know, Mrs Jenkins. We'd want you once a week and when we have parties. Later on when we start a family—' she had blushed at the looks both Mrs Jenkins and Ben had given her.

At last Mrs Jenkins had departed still clutching her precious key as proof of her re-entry in due course.

'Whew! I don't know how they ever managed in the

old days with servants hovering to anticipate their slightest wish. Come here, darling, and give me a kiss. I need some reassurance after that lot!'

It was only later they got back down to their planning. Apart from redecorating and things like brighter curtains there wasn't going to be so much after all.

'Sure you feel all right about it, Lynne?'

'Yes, I do now. I wasn't sure at first as I kept expecting to see Aunt Jenny walk in. Once the painters have finished it will be our own place, and after all, she wouldn't have left it to us if she hadn't wanted us to be happy here.'

'She left it to you,' Ben insisted.

Lynne shook her head. 'You're wrong, darling. The will wasn't made until *after* she had met you, so she must have approved.'

'Perhaps she thought you would be sharing it with old Timothy,' Ben said a trifle jealously.

Lynne put her arms around him. 'Don't ever say that again! Timothy was connected with *her* past, not with *my* future!'

Christmas descended upon them with a thud. There were all the decorations to put up, the wards to help as their own work load decreased slightly. Lynne couldn't remember when she had enjoyed a Christmas more whether it was their candlelit carol procession round the wards with the snow falling softly outside, or the parties on the wards, in the common rooms, or the snatched moments in a quiet corner, the sluice room, or the linen room.

Perhaps Sister Casualty summed it up for all of them. 'I've never known such a happy time. I'm going to miss it all.'

Ben struck a cheerful note. 'We'll have to bring you back to cover time off for having babies!'

Everyone joined in shouting him down. 'Stop rushing us, Ben! We haven't even had our honeymoons yet!'

Then almost before they had time to catch their breaths December had given way to January. February had followed with its bitter winds and treacherous frosts. March lambs had scarcely bleated before there were final fittings for dresses, frantic scannings of lists, gloatings over piles of lovely presents, last-minute plan alterations.

Bibs and Peter Grant were the first to be launched, and Lynne had never seen a girl look happier as the new Mrs Grant walked down the aisle with her husband. She wiped away a tear and even Ben looked misty-eyed. Another fortnight and it would be their turn.

Ben surveyed the reception room after the honeymooners had been duly dispatched. 'What a shambles! Is ours going to be like this?'

Lynne slipped her hand into his. 'At least we won't ever know—we'll be catching our plane! It's the people left behind who clear up. We'll come back to a warm house, aired beds, and Mrs Jenkins hovering!'

'*One* aired bed, sweetie, and don't you dare let Mrs Jenkins hover! I want you all to myself, so there!'

Lynne soothed him, 'She'll go the moment we arrive—but of course if you'd rather have frozen pipes and a chilly house?'

Ben groaned. 'At Easter? Maybe you're right, darling. I'll be glad when it's all over.'

'Ben! We're only getting married once, so let's enjoy it! I know I'm going to.'

Ben put his arm across her shoulders. 'No doubt, darling? There's still time to change your mind—'

Lynne's eyes widened. 'Ben, you don't want—'

Regardless of the maids clearing the tables, Ben swept

her into his arms and kissed her until she was breathless. 'I was only playing fair—' he growled softly. 'Oh, Lynne, if anything happened I'd cry buckets!'

'Doctors don't cry,' Lynne reminded him, her own voice trembling a little.

'There can always be a first time—'

Their wedding day dawned with a threat of clouds that soon vanished under the brisk touch of a crisp breeze. The ends of Lynne's veil were whisked briefly into a cascade of white froth as she got out of the car and took her father's arm. The crowds of people waiting and the ragged cheer that ran through the ranks made her realise that not only guests had come to wish her well. These were patients, nurses, maids and porters—or just passers-by caught up in the excitement of a wedding.

Lynne's heart slowed its excited beating a fraction as she saw Ben and his best man waiting for them. At the right moment Sarah Wishart took Lynne's bouquet and smiled a secret little smile at Timothy Lawson—Ben's best man—but her own husband-to-be. The little bridesmaids and the page boy made the right moves— and then Lynne was standing beside Ben and her own new life—*their* new life—was about to begin.

Walking back down the church on Ben's arm Lynne caught a glimpse of Sister Casualty unashamedly mopping her eyes and yet smiling at the same instant. It all seemed such an unbelievable dream and it was happening to her—to them.

As they stepped into the car Lynne caught a glimpse of two children alike as two peas gaily holding up bandaged hands to cheer them on. 'It's the terrible twins, Ben!'

'Forget about them, Mrs Gresham!' Ben ordered sternly. 'They'll still be around when we get back from our honeymoon—you can count on that.'

Lynne could never be sure which good wishes she

would treasure the most—parents—relatives—staff—patients—the Jenkins family complete for once—or even the stewardess's kind welcome as she strapped them into their seats.

'We call this the Honeymoon Special. May all your landings be happy ones!'

The plane took off and lifted smoothly into the cold blue sky and the sun touched the frost crystals on the wings—the scattering of snow on the higher hills—

Lynne and Ben held hands tightly until the plane levelled out. He bent over and unfastened her belt and then his own.

'Darling—I'm so happy—are you?'

The expression in her eyes was answer enough. 'Oh, Ben!'